The Betrayal

ERIN MCCAULEY

Author of *The Confession* and *The Truth*

CRIMSON
ROMANCE

F+W Media, Inc.

Published by
Crimson Romance
an imprint of F+W Media, Inc.
10151 Carver Road, Suite 200
Blue Ash, OH 45242. U.S.A.
www.crimsonromance.com

ISBN 10: 1-4405-5420-X
ISBN 13: 978-1-4405-5420-9
eISBN 10: 1-4405-5421-8
eISBN 13: 978-1-4405-5421-6

Cover art © 123rf.com/Steve Everts

For all my girls starting a new chapter in their life.

May we all find our Happily Ever After.

Acknowledgments

I have to give a huge thank you to my editor, Julie. I couldn't have completed this book without you. Your insight, understanding, and your sense of humor have been invaluable to me these last few months.

I have to say a special thank you to Tammy Smith, for the hours spent in my office reading and re-reading the same pages over and over again until I got them right. For sitting by the phone until two in the morning to make sure I met my deadline, and always being there when I need you. We make a great team and I love you from the bottom of my heart.

To my readers, thank you for your patience and for your continued support. I couldn't do any of this without you.

Chapter 1

It had been six days since Marissa had heard from her husband, and she couldn't sleep. She poured water from the kettle over the tea bag and mindlessly dunked it up and down. It was hard enough to hold a marriage together, but over the last four years, his architectural firm had him working in the city almost full time and his trips home had become less frequent.

She worried Steven would show up one day and tell her they were moving to the city. She loved living in Carmel; the quaint little shops, the slower pace, and the friendly people, not to mention she loved her house and the fact the beach was just down the street. Besides, her job was here, and her patients needed her. When she told people she was a nurse at a hospice house, they almost always scrunched their faces and looked at her like she was crazy, but she felt she was making a difference. Helping people in their lowest moments, when they were searching for peace and needing to share the memories they cherished most with anyone who would listen. In some ways, they helped her more than she helped them. She held their hands, held water to their lips, and listened as they reminisced; each story touched her. Each one a lesson of sorts she could use to ensure her own happiness.

The knock on the door startled her and tea sloshed over the rim of her cup. She looked up at the clock on the wall; it was three-thirty in the morning. Walking to the door, she slid back the curtain and peered out, surprised to see Jordan. He was in his police uniform; his face somber, and nervously wringing his hands.

Flipping the lock, she pulled her robe closed and opened the door.

"I know it's late," he said, his deep green eyes shadowed and apologetic.

"What's happened? Is it Lexie?" Her heart raced.

He shook his head, and swallowed hard. "Can we sit down?"

His nervousness made her uneasy. She'd known Jordan for most of her life. Not only had he been her first love, but his sister, Lexie, was her best friend. Knowing him the way she did, the news he'd brought wasn't good.

She followed him into the kitchen and waited anxiously while he removed his hat and jacket and laid them neatly over one of the open stools at the breakfast bar. She concentrated on pulling air into her lungs and blowing it out slowly, struggling to remain silent while waiting for him to speak.

He folded his tall frame onto the stool beside her, and reached over to take her hand. Looking into his handsome, familiar face, she felt her blood rush when she saw the tears pooling in his eyes. She'd never seen Jordan cry.

"Jordan, you're scaring me. What's going on?" she asked.

He lowered his head, concentrating on their joined hands. Without looking up, he whispered, "It's Steven."

It took a moment for his words to sink in. "What about Steven?" she asked, lifting his chin with her free hand, forcing him to look at her. "Jordan, tell me what's happened."

"There was an accident." His eyes locked with hers. "I'm so sorry. He's dead, Marissa."

She felt the warmth of the tears roll down her cheeks, but the rest of her body was numb. Unseeing, she continued to stare at Jordan. Her tongue felt glued behind her teeth, the questions flowing through her mind remained there as her throat constricted, striking her mute.

Jordan gently wiped the tears from her cheeks. "Marissa, there's more." He cleared his throat and picked up her now cold cup of tea and took a large swallow. "Shit," he spat, and climbing down from the stool, began to pace. "Why did I think I should be the one to do this?" he mumbled. "Shit, shit, shit."

Marissa narrowed her eyes and stood to block his path. "What do you mean there's more?" she asked, scared into finding her voice.

His expressive face changed like a slide show from frustration to pity to sadness. He grasped her elbow and tried to lead her back to the stool. "Here, let's sit back down," he suggested.

Surprised by her own reaction, she jerked her arm back, and stood rigid before him. "No! I won't sit! Just tell me what's going on, Jordan Wayne. Just tell me."

He closed his eyes, and said, "He wasn't alone in the car."

Marissa felt the air burst from her lungs, and grabbed for the stool to catch her balance. She knew the answer before she asked the question but asked anyway. "Was he with another woman?"

Jordan nodded his head, watching her intently.

Needing to keep her hands busy, she walked on shaky legs around the breakfast bar and put the kettle back on the burner. Without looking at him, she pulled another mug from the cupboard.

"She didn't make it either," Jordan informed her.

Placing a tea bag in the mug, she reached over and turned off the burner. Leaning against the counter, Marissa lowered her head and struggled to control the tears. Was she sad or angry? Both, she guessed.

She heard Jordan approach but couldn't lift her head to acknowledge him. He placed his hand on her shoulder, and she tilted her head to rest her cheek against it, seeping in the comfort he offered. Gently he turned her to face him. She lifted her chin, and looked into his concerned eyes.

"I'm sorry I snapped at you."

A corner of his mouth began to twitch. "Only you, Marissa Neil, would be worried about offending me at a time like this."

"Good manners are important," she said, grateful for the break in the tension.

He pulled a glass from the cupboard and walked to the other end of the kitchen before handing it to her. She recoiled in surprise at the strong scent of straight whiskey. "You're going to need this," he told her, wrapping her fingers around the glass and urging her to drink.

Taking a large sip, she let the warmth flow through her, even as she scrunched her nose at the harsh flavor. Jordan poured a bit more into her glass, picked up one he'd poured for himself, and led her into the living room.

He sat on the sofa and patted the cushion beside him. She could tell by the look in his eyes he was holding something back.

Sitting down, she took another swallow and set the glass on the table. What else could there be? Her mind raced with worst case scenarios but none of them came close to the news she'd received in the last hour. Time seemed to stand still as he remained silent. She was beginning to feel she'd go crazy if he didn't just come out with it. Turning to him she urged, "What is it?" When his silence continued she reached out and took hold of his free hand. "This must be relatively easy after the news you've already told me." She was surprised when he shook his head no. "What else could there possibly be? My husband was having an affair, and I find out because he died with her. What could possibly be worse than that?"

Jordan downed his glass, turned to her, and grabbed both of her hands. Taking a deep breath, he blew it out slowly, the tangy scent of whiskey floating between them. "Her name was Jane Neil." He paused, waiting for her reaction.

"Neil? That's a strange coincidence." Marissa thought for a moment, then added, "Do you know her?"

Jordan shook his head. "And it's not a coincidence. According to the LA County records, she was his wife."

Marissa felt like the wind had been knocked out of her. Wife? How was that possible?

"They've been married for four years, although now it will come out it wasn't a legal marriage because he was already married to you."

She sat in silence, tears wetting her cheeks as she tried to process what he was saying. Her head swirled with confusion and disbelief. She stood and paced, sat back down, and stood again. Jordan sat silently watching her. Her eyes drew together, and she could feel the color seeping into her cheeks. Her heart rate increased, each beat feeling as though it would burst through her chest.

"That's a lie! The records are wrong," she shouted. "Steven wasn't capable of what you're saying." She could feel the rage now pouring through her.

"Marissa—"

"You're wrong," she snapped.

His voice rose, demanding her attention. "They have a two-year-old daughter."

"Get out!" She wrapped her arms around herself rocking back and forth on her heels. Her stomach churned, as the whiskey threatened to escape. It had to be a lie. It was enough to learn her husband had died, but to discover she'd never known him at all? It was just too much. She couldn't believe it. She wouldn't believe it.

"Marissa…"

She held up her hand. She didn't want him to speak; she simply wanted him to tell her it wasn't true.

"Jordan, please," she spoke softly, "please go home and leave me alone. I just want to be alone."

She turned away without looking at him and raced from the room.

Chapter 2

Exhausted but unable to sleep, Marissa climbed out of bed only three hours later. She wasn't surprised to find Jordan asleep on her couch, nor was she was shocked to find Lexie making coffee in her kitchen.

She came around the counter and wrapped Marissa in her arms. "I'm so sorry. What a bastard. If he weren't already dead, I'd..." She lowered her head, clearly stopping herself from finishing her thought. "Sorry, bad timing. I'm just so angry. How're you holding up?"

Marissa shrugged her shoulders and scooted up on the stool, accepting the steaming cup of coffee Lexie handed her.

"I take it Jordan called you?"

She nodded her head. "He didn't know whether to leave you alone, or be there if you needed him. That and he finished the rest of your whiskey, so he couldn't drive."

In normal circumstances, Marissa would have laughed. Lexie always made her laugh. She wondered if she'd ever be able to even smile again.

"Do you think it's true?" Marissa asked hesitantly. "That Steven had another wife and a child?"

"I know Jordan verified everything before telling you." Lexie wrapped a comforting arm around Marissa's shoulder. "He would never want to hurt you if it was avoidable."

She knew her friend was right, and felt horrible for shouting at him last night.

"Me too," said a groggy voice. "Coffee." Jordan walked into the kitchen wearing his t-shirt and the wrinkled khakis from his uniform and slid onto the stool beside her, studying her in silence.

"You didn't have to stay," she told him, and turning to Lexie, added, "You shouldn't have left your family to come here. I'm fine."

"You're not fine," Lexie said matter-of-factly. "How could you be?" Lexie poured herself a cup and hopped onto the counter beside them. "And I thought you might want my help with the funeral arrangements."

She hadn't even thought about that. If she were to be honest with herself, she didn't want to think about it. She clenched her fists and felt the blood pumping through her veins. "They can bury him in an unmarked grave, feed him to the piranhas, or let the vultures have him. I really don't care."

"I know how hard this must be for—"

"No, you don't!" Marissa snapped. "You have no idea. Neither of you do."

Lexie looked at her sympathetically. "You're right, we don't. I can only imagine how much this is to process, and I'm so sorry you're going through it, but we have to talk about what happens now. You have some choices to make and not a lot of time to make them."

"Lexie, I can't do this now. I can't think about Steven's funeral. I'm angry at him—no, not angry, I'm livid." Marissa ran her hand through her hair and shook her head. "How is this even happening? How do you get past being betrayed this way? Being humiliated and made a fool of?"

"He's the fool, not you," Jordan spoke softly.

"Jordan's right. What Steven did to you is unforgiveable, but sadly it doesn't change the fact that you have some major decisions you have to make." Lexie looked apologetic. "Have you thought about Chloe? What your decision might be?"

"Who?"

"Steven's daughter."

"What decision?" Marissa asked, confused by the question. Watching the looks pitched back and forth between brother and sister, she pursed her lips. "What is it?" her voice cracked.

Jordan gave his sister another glare before giving Marissa his attention. He swallowed hard and blurted, "Steven left a request for you to raise his daughter if anything happened to him."

Marissa felt her stomach roil and an overwhelming urge to be sick. This was all too much. "Me?" She leapt from the stool and stared incredulously at him. "I didn't even know she existed before last night. Why would he do that?"

She flung her cup at the wall, knocking the hanging antique clock to the floor. She sneered as it shattered into tiny splinters. It had been a gift from Steven on their third wedding anniversary. With a satisfied grunt, she marched from the kitchen.

She watched from her bedroom window as her friends climbed into their cars and drove away. An overwhelming sense of relief washed over her. She wanted to feel sorry for herself, to hide from the world and pretend this wasn't happening. She wanted to turn back time to yesterday, the week before, maybe even as far back as the day she first laid eyes on Steven Neil. It was just like him to create this monumental mess and leave her to clean it up. Selfish ass. She hunched her shoulders and crossed her arms trying to control her shaking. Sobs racked her body, and a feeling of hopelessness overwhelmed her.

She wanted to lash out, break something, punch someone; anything to relieve the pressure in her chest and the pain in her heart.

Raising her hand to wipe her eyes, she stopped abruptly and stared at her left hand. The simple gold band wrapped around her finger mocked her and filled her with rage. She flung open the window, tugged the ring from her finger, and threw it as hard as she could into the wind.

Chapter 3

Collapsing onto the bed, Marissa pulled the covers to her chin, and tried to shut her mind off. Her body was heavy with fatigue, her head pounded, and her eyes burned. *Damn you, Steven. Why couldn't you have just left me? Set me free to live my life.* She could have handled his leaving her for another woman—hell, she wouldn't have even been surprised. But to keep her anchored in a charade of a marriage, knowing he had no intention of keeping true to any of his vows, was cruel and selfish.

In retrospect she shouldn't have been surprised he'd been seeing another woman. She'd known Steven didn't love her the way he used to—if at all—and somewhere in the last three years, probably closer to five if she were to be honest, she'd fallen out of love with him.

And yet Steven knew she wouldn't have left him. No matter how bad things were, she'd made a promise, and she never would have broken it. Her father left her and her mother when Marissa was only six years old. For the next ten years she watched her mother drink herself to death. The only promise her mother ever asked of her was to take marriage seriously. She'd kept that promise, even after recognizing she'd married the wrong man.

She once believed it would be Jordan she'd marry. At eighteen years old, did anyone really know what real love was? Besides, if Jordan was the one, how could she have fallen so easily for Steven? And she had to admit she'd fallen hard. He'd been smart, funny, sexy, and charismatic. His steel blue eyes locked with hers and she'd believed everything she'd ever dreamed of was standing before her.

He'd told her he wanted a house full of children, a dog, and the white picket fence. He lied. By their first anniversary, Steven had already immersed himself in his career, spending most of his time in the Los Angeles office. When she'd realized how distant they were becoming, she'd even once offered to transfer and move to be with him, but he'd assured her it was only temporary. He lied about that, too. Every time she'd brought up having children he'd dismiss the idea, stating the time wasn't right. After eight years of marriage, the timing had never been right. She supposed for Steven, it would've been difficult having children with both of his wives. She choked back a sarcastic laugh. At least she'd stopped crying.

She threw back the covers and walked into the bathroom for a drink of water. Opening the medicine cabinet for the bottle of aspirin, she stilled. Anger surged through her as she scanned the contents: Steven's toothbrush, deodorant, favorite cologne, shaving cream, razor. Fueled with rage, she grabbed the trash can and swiped the bottles from Steven's shelf into the bin. She pulled open the drawers, and emptied them, tossing out his comb, his aftershave, his hair gel, and even his extra pack of cotton swabs. When the garbage can was full, she rushed downstairs and grabbed the box of trash bags from the pantry.

She felt crazed, energized, and yet somehow soothed. She hurried back up to the bedroom and emptied Steven's dresser drawers, his closet, and even his nightstand. She dragged the bags down the steps two at a time, and left them on the curb for the garbage truck. Wearing only her nightgown, she ignored the damp grass beneath her feet as she made trip after trip to the street.

Spotting her wedding picture sitting on the shelf in the foyer, she growled, her fury boiling to the surface again. Picking up the photo, she marched through the first floor, stacking pictures in her arms as she removed every last photograph with Steven in it. Having run out of trash bags, she dropped the stack of pictures onto the sidewalk, pleased with the sound of shattering glass.

Parading back into the house, she threw open the door to Steven's den. She hated this room. It was always cluttered and dusty, but he forbade her to touch it. She couldn't even remember the last time he'd been home long enough to step foot inside this room. Now she knew why.

Narrowing her eyes, she stared at the wall of football trophies. Clenching her fist, she yanked the large leather chair from behind the wooden desk, crossed the room, and with one swipe, cleared the shelf, sending the trophies crashing onto the seat of the chair and the floor around it.

Pushing it out of the room, she stopped at the front door and tipped the chair, letting the trophies fall to the porch with a loud crash before pulling it back down the hall again.

• • •

Jordan groaned as he pulled up to Marissa's house. Her neighbor had called into the station to report a crazy woman running around in her nightgown, dumping household items on her lawn. She hadn't been exaggerating.

Trash bags overflowed and clothes spilled out onto the sidewalk. Shattered glass was strewn everywhere, and walking to the porch, he stepped over piles of broken trophies, smashed frames, and even a bashed in computer monitor. Stepping inside the open door, he followed the sound of more items breaking down the hall.

His own heart broke when he reached what remained of Steven's den. Marissa was pulling papers from filing cabinets and tossing them in a pile around a chair. Her eyes were wild, her cheeks stained with tears, and what appeared to be small cuts on her legs were still bleeding. It didn't seem like she'd noticed.

Stepping over to her, he placed his hands on her shoulders. Obviously she hadn't known he was there because she lept in surprise. Her mouth turned down, and her eyes threw daggers at him. Apparently she wasn't in the mood to be interrupted.

"Marissa, this isn't going to help anything," he told her calmly, meeting her crazed gaze.

"That's where you're wrong, Jordan, or is it Officer Wayne?" she snapped and jerked her shoulders from his grip. "If you are here to arrest me, go ahead—if not, get out of my way."

Walking around him, she started to push the chair from the room.

"Marissa," he shouted. "Enough!"

She froze, her back hunched, and she slowly turned around to face him. Her eyes were no longer glazed and the redness in her cheeks was fading. He took a large step toward her and pulled her into his arms, holding her as she sobbed against his chest.

He tipped his head down and kissed the top of her head. The floral scent of her hair pulled at him, reminding him of happier days. He remembered her as a young girl, happy and carefree. Nothing like the heartbroken, angry woman she was now. In high school he'd watched her walk the halls, giggling with her friends, her auburn hair always tied back in a long pony tail. He recalled the way her hair felt against his hands the first time he'd loosened it from its band and dug his hands into its silken mass. The shy way she'd looked at him when he'd pulled her closer and they shared their first kiss. He could still taste her, all these years later. There had been so many times he'd wished he'd chosen to go to college with her instead of joining the police academy. Maybe she wouldn't have met Steven.

Jerking back, he shook his head. Why was he reminiscing now? It'd been ten years since she'd been his. Now she was his friend, and only his friend. She needed him in the present, not thinking like a teenage boy with a crush.

He could feel the moment she'd exhausted herself, and gently lifting her into his arms, he carried her up the stairs and laid her on the bed. Walking into the bathroom, he dampened a towel and when he returned, he found her already asleep. He gently washed the blood from her legs and tucked the covers around her.

Picking up the few remaining pieces of Steven's things, he closed the door behind him and headed downstairs. He hated to see her this way. What Steven had done to her was unforgiveable. What he feared most was causing her the same amount of anger and pain with what he'd done. He knew he'd do everything in his power to keep that from happening.

He picked up the phone and called in a favor. "I need you to come to Marissa's, and bring the truck."

Chapter 4

Marissa's footsteps echoed through the hall as she made her way to the office of Diane Williams, Chloe's caseworker with Child Protective Services. She stopped outside the door, wiped her sweaty palms on her skirt, and straightened her back. With a shaky hand, she reached for the door handle, then quickly regretted her decision to do this alone.

Both Jordan and Lexie had volunteered to come with her, but she'd insisted she would be fine. In one week's time she'd buried her husband and discovered divorce papers in his belongings, as well as a photocopy of a document requesting she raise Chloe if anything were to happen to him. What she hadn't found was any sort of understanding. Why would he marry Jane when he was already married to her? Why had it taken him this long to ask for a divorce? And why would he feel justified in asking her to care for his daughter?

It was all happening so quickly. She was still unsure if she'd made the right decision to take Chloe in. Would she feel resentment toward the little girl, knowing she was the other woman's child? She'd always thought she'd be a great mother, but now that it was a reality, she questioned herself. Would she be able to love her the way a mother should?

It was Lexie who'd convinced her to take this step. She'd reminded her that everything happened for a reason and even convinced Marissa she'd never forgive herself if a child fell into the system because she was afraid. Lexie was right, she couldn't let that happen. It wasn't Chloe's fault her father was a liar and a cheat. As angry as she was at Steven, she couldn't take it out on an innocent child. She understood too well the pain of losing both parents at a young age.

Squeezing her eyes shut, Marissa took one final deep breath and opened the door. Ms. Williams looked up from a stack of papers she'd been shuffling through and smiled.

"You must be Marissa Neil," she said, coming around the desk to shake her hand. "Everything's in order. Your paperwork has been filed, the judge has approved temporary guardianship, and your court date has been set for request of permanent custody should you choose it. These are your copies." She handed an envelope to Marissa. "You and I will pick up Chloe first thing tomorrow. In the meantime, you'll need a car seat. Do you have the key to their residence?"

Marissa's head was spinning. Her mouth fell open, but no words came out. Did she have a key to whose residence? A car seat? She hadn't thought of these things. Was the child still in diapers at two? Would she need a crib, or would the small bed she'd purchased and put into the guest room be appropriate?

She looked into Ms. Williams' understanding gaze, and apparently confusion was written all over her face because the caseworker added, "If you don't have a key, you should be able to get in with a copy of your guardianship papers."

"Get in where?"

"I thought it might be helpful for you to pick up some of Chloe's things. It would make the transition easier for her because she will have some sense of the familiar, and for you, because you haven't had to shop for a two-year-old before now."

Marissa felt a new wave of panic race through her, and she grabbed hold of the chair to steady herself. "You mean go to Steven's house? His house with Jane?"

"Are you alright? You've gone completely white." Ms. Williams made a tsking sound as she pulled over a chair and lowered Marissa carefully onto the padded seat. "If you'd like, you could wait in the hall while I gather some of Chloe's things for you. Would that be easier?"

Marissa managed to nod her head. The thought of even standing in the hallway was overwhelming.

"I've got a free hour now," the caseworker told her. "Think you can handle this?"

She didn't, but Marissa agreed, picked up her purse, and followed Ms. Williams out of the office.

Pulling up to the front of the complex in West Hollywood, her chest constricted and her mind filled with visions of Steven pushing a baby stroller and holding hands with another woman. It was like a bad dream she couldn't wake from.

Marissa concentrated on breathing in and out to slow down her racing heart. Believing she could finally stand without her knees buckling, she stepped from the car and looked up at the massive building that contained Steven and Jane's condo. Her mouth dropped open. She'd seen this building before. This was one of Steven's buildings. She'd watched him construct the scale model and remembered thinking it was too cold, too much steel, and no place she'd choose to live. Of course she'd never said it aloud to him, but the thought of him moving in here with his other wife was painful and felt malicious.

The entry allowed a clear view of the lobby and its continued use of modern glass and steel. Catching sight of the engraved steel sign, she gasped and turned to the caseworker.

"What did you say Jane Neil's maiden name was?"

"Smith, why?"

Marissa felt the pain slice through her as she read the sign again. Steven had named it The Smithton Towers.

Unable to speak, she shook her head, and entered the cool lobby. Side by side with Ms. Williams, they approached the clerk behind the front desk.

He was a tall, dark-haired man with a flawlessly tanned face and sparkling white teeth. "Good afternoon, ladies, welcome to The Smithton. How can I help you?"

"I'm Marissa Neil, and I need access to one of your tenant's homes. Mr. Neil has recently passed—"

"It's horrible! I'm still in shock. Such a wonderful couple; taken way too soon. And that poor baby girl..." The man laid his hand over his heart.

Marissa tried to control the shiver that shook her body. Thankfully, Ms. Williams stepped forward and showed the clerk her badge. "Mrs. Neil is going to be taking care of Chloe, and she needs to pick up a few items. We have the paperwork proving she is the court approved guardian. Do you think you could assist us?"

The clerk's eyes grew misty. "Let me place a call to my supervisor. I'm sure we can work this out for Chloe's sake."

By unspoken agreement, the two women headed to a section of black leather chairs to wait for clearance.

Fifteen minutes later, they stood outside the unlocked door of condo 17-101. Ms. Williams, true to her word, started to shut the door after she entered, leaving Marissa in the hallway and closing off the view.

Marissa couldn't get the picture of Steven in his den moving walls and adding bathrooms to blueprints of this building out of her mind. Had he been designing it for Jane all along? The few times he'd asked her opinion had he been mocking her? Secretly laughing at what a fool she was?

Clenching her fists, and embracing her anger, she muttered, "Wait, I'm coming with you."

The interior appeared to have been decorated by the same designer as the lobby. The large living area boasted a red suede sofa set on a thick, white fur throw rug. The tables were glass and chrome, and a chrome lamp reached over the seating area like a giant claw. Her eyes were drawn to a large, silver frame atop a black lacquer shelf, and Marissa walked on wooden legs across the cold slate floor until the black-and-white photo was the only thing that filled her vision.

Steven gazed lovingly at a petite blonde in an elegant lace wedding gown. Her eyes shone with the joy of a bride on her big day, her head tilted up, a large diamond ring flashing on her left hand. Marissa felt her chest tighten and the air burst from her lungs as if she'd been kicked in the stomach. She jolted when she felt a comforting hand rest on her shoulder.

"Are you sure you wouldn't rather wait in the hallway?" Ms. Williams asked her in a compassionate tone.

She shook her head. "It feels so cold." She gestured at the room with her arm. "It's so very different from our home." She felt the tears well, and tilted her head to stop their flow. "My home," she corrected.

The caseworker placed an arm across Marissa's shoulders and led her from the room, away from the photograph that held her glued in place. They walked past the kitchen with its black granite counters and chrome appliances. The only sign of a child was a high chair beside the glass-topped kitchen table. The woman steered her down a hallway off the kitchen. The walls were bare, white, and long.

With the exception of the sofa, Chloe's bedroom was the first sign of color Marissa had seen since she'd entered the house. The walls were cotton candy pink, the furniture white wood. Happy, bright-colored butterflies flew across the walls, and stuffed giraffes, elephants, and bears filled the corner. She turned at the sound of a low whistle.

Ms. Williams stood in the open closet door. Joining her, Marissa peeked inside, sucking in a breath. The closet seemed to go on forever. Racks filled with baby clothes ran along both sides, and floor-to-ceiling shelves were lined with little hats, shoes, and folded sweaters. It looked like a department store, not a two-year-old's closet.

"I don't think you'll need to do much shopping." Ms. Williams' sarcastic tone made Marissa giggle. "I try not to judge, but this closet alone could clothe half the foster kids in LA."

Marissa walked inside and pulled a Coach diaper bag from one of the shelves. "Let's grab a few things, and I promise you, if I'm granted permanent custody, you will have a large delivery coming your way for those foster kids. Besides, I like shopping."

The other woman smiled appreciatively, and began to pick a few items from the hangers and shelves. Marissa excused herself; she needed a moment to calm her frayed nerves and splash some cold water on her face.

She located the bathroom further down the hallway, but her attention was suddenly diverted toward the closed door at the end of the hall. Turning, she walked hesitantly to it, her hand hovering above the knob. With a decisive move, she swooped down to grip the handle and throw open the door, revealing the master bedroom.

Marissa scanned the large room, her heart beating faster as she took notice of the large bed with tall, thick, black posts and a white comforter. Like the rest of the house, no color existed; only neutrals, metal, and glass. Desperately trying to avoid mental images of Steven lying beside another woman, she noticed his familiar reading glasses on a glass table beside the bed atop a stack of papers. She found no comfort in the fact that he worked in their bedroom, too, while Jane tried to sleep.

She turned to leave and froze when she noticed another photo set on the dresser. Straightening her back and pushing aside her sudden rage, she walked to the familiar picture in a frame she'd given her husband for Christmas years ago. It was the same picture of Steven's parents that had sat on his desk in her home. She hadn't noticed it missing. If she'd needed any other proof he was choosing to leave her for wife number two, this was it. His most prized possession was no longer in their home together; instead it sat symbolically in his other life.

Wiping the tears from her cheeks, she picked up the photograph and left the room, leaving a small part of her pride behind as she closed the door behind her. She met Ms. Williams in the hall and without explanation, placed the photograph in a pocket of one of the bags the woman carried.

She paused, taking one last look around the cold, sterile home her husband had chosen instead of the cozy home she'd lovingly built with him in hopes of filling it with children. Her heart beat heavy against her chest when she spotted a small hand print toward the bottom of the clean, shiny chrome refrigerator.

Chapter 5

The following morning, Marissa stood nervously on the sidewalk outside of a small time-worn house, surrounded by a rickety chain link fence. Sounds of children laughing and an infant crying drifted out of the small, open windows. She wiped her sweaty hands on her shorts and straightened the cotton blouse she wore. After a sleepless night, and this morning's anticipation, she felt like a dry twig about to snap. She couldn't remember a time she'd felt so anxious.

Ms. Williams stood beside her, smiling in that knowing way Marissa recognized. "It's going to be fine," she reassured her. "Trust me."

Marissa wished she had the same confidence. Instead, her heart raced, her hands shook, and she couldn't breathe. What if Chloe didn't like her? What if she couldn't do this? But deep down, she knew it was too late to rethink it now.

With one last deep inhale, she walked through the metal gate and up the cracked cement steps.

The large Hispanic woman who opened the door appeared frazzled. Her shirt was askew and covered in what appeared to be breakfast, and her hair was falling from its clip and standing in three separate directions. The baby she held against her hip had been the crying infant they'd heard, her little face red from the effort. When the woman realized who was at the door, her smile was genuine and lit her entire face. Somehow, it put Marissa at ease.

"Come in, come in," she welcomed in a strong Mexican accent. "Excuse the mess, the children are full of energy this morning, and even more full of naughtiness."

The caseworker introduced the two women, and Marissa held out her hand, grinning as she realized Maria didn't have a free one.

She was amazed by the number of children filling the small living area. Three young boys sat on the worn sofa, arguing over a video game controller, and two young girls sat cross-legged on the floor playing with Barbie dolls. Maria set the infant on the floor, and Marissa watched as she crawled directly toward the girls. In a matter of seconds, the girls were raising their voices at the baby, and she immediately began to cry again. How did Maria handle this day after day?

As if reading her mind, Ms. Williams whispered, "She's a saint. I don't know how she does it."

Marissa nodded, waiting while Maria calmed the commotion. As she watched, a small, shy girl peeked from around the sofa. Her blonde curls appeared feather soft and fell delicately across her lowered forehead. But it was her eyes that held Marissa captive. Steven's steel blue eyes peered curiously beneath long lashes, watching her intently.

Her heart skipped a beat as the hesitant little girl took a step toward her, coming out of her hiding place. With her head down, she slowly took another step, then another. To Marissa, it felt like they were the only two in the room as she knelt down, silently willing Chloe to come to her. With cautious steps, Chloe made her way until she stood silently in front of her. Without hesitation, Marissa held open her arms and sighed with relief as Chloe came into them and wrapped her tiny arms around Marissa's neck.

She felt a warmth run through her. A feeling she couldn't quite identify, and never felt before. Marissa held her a little tighter, trying to block the image of this fragile, innocent little girl alone in a state facility. Thankfully she'd made the right choice in caring for her and she'd spend the rest of her life making up for the moments she'd doubted her decision.

When she stood again with Chloe clinging tightly to her, she noticed every eye in the room was on them. Maria broke the silence and muttered, "I'll be, that precious *chica* wouldn't let any of us hold her."

The caseworker breathed an audible sigh of relief. "See, I told you it would be fine."

With Chloe still clinging tightly, Marissa managed to open the car trunk to store Chloe's few belongings from her foster home and unlock the driver side door. Maria bent over and kissed Chloe on the cheek before walking back inside to deal with another loud fight over the game controller.

"Will you be alright?" Ms. Williams asked.

"I have to be," she said as she placed Chloe in her new car seat. The toddler reached out for her as she backed out of the doorframe but didn't cry or fuss. "I'm right here," Marissa reassured, handing Chloe a stuffed ladybug she hadn't been able to resist buying. Pulling the stuffed animal closer, the child settled back, never taking her eyes from Marissa.

"She is sure taken with you already," Ms. Williams said, watching the interaction. "Remember, you can call me anytime, day or night."

"Thanks. For everything," Marissa leaned in, giving her a hug before climbing behind the wheel for their long trip back to Carmel. For a moment she wondered if she should have flown after all.

With one last look over her shoulder at Chloe, who was now sound asleep in her seat, and a final wave out the open window, she placed the car in drive and headed home with her new daughter.

Chapter 6

It had been a rough couple of days. Deep down, Jordan felt like a heel for not accompanying Marissa to Los Angeles, despite her protests. That's what friends were for, to stand beside each other and hold her up if she needed him. Although he knew she wouldn't. She was, and had always been, the strongest woman he knew.

Done with his shift, he closed the door to his office and headed out to meet Grayson. His partner was now his brother-in-law but also a good friend. A beer and a game of pool was exactly what he wanted tonight.

"You ready?" Jordan tapped on the open office door.

Grayson looked regretful. "I can't tonight."

"Let me guess, ball and chain revoke your parole?"

Grayson laughed. "Not at all, Lexie's just offering up something *much* better than a beer with you." He winked and grabbed for his keys.

"How many times do I have to tell you I don't want to ever hear about you and my sister? That is wrong man, just wrong." He made a cartoonish grimace. "Besides, you and I both know who wears the pants at your house."

"There are too many ways I can knock you down right now. But knowing how sad and pathetic your lonely life is, I'm going to leave this one alone." He mockingly patted Jordan on the shoulder and walked away.

He couldn't argue his life was pathetic, and he supposed inside he was jealous. He wanted to be rushing home to someone. At one point in his life he was certain that person would be Marissa. She'd been unhappy about his decision to forego college and instead follow in the footsteps of the men in his family and join the police academy. He'd worried about the time they'd be apart and how two young kids, no matter how in love they'd thought they were, would keep a long distance relationship strong for four years. By the end of her first year at Boston University, he'd already noticed her drifting away. She'd sworn it was her workload and the time difference, but deep down he'd known. It wasn't long after that he'd received the call she'd met Steven.

He tried not to think about the what-ifs. Steven was the night to his day and Jordan couldn't grasp how she'd loved them both. But she'd made her choice, and it wasn't him, so he'd been her friend, and would continue to be.

Now that his plans with Grayson had changed, maybe he'd head over to Marissa's place, meet Chloe, and fix them both a homemade meal. That's what friends did. Decision made, he put his truck in gear and headed for the grocery store.

An hour later he had spaghetti sauce simmering on the stove, a fresh loaf of French bread ready to be cut, and a salad chilling in the refrigerator next to a nice bottle of wine. He'd also picked up a box of Cheerios, some bananas, and a bottle of apple juice for Chloe.

He'd just curled up on her couch to catch the news when he heard the car pull up in the driveway. Stepping out on the porch, he watched while she opened the passenger door and lifted a tiny blonde girl from inside. He could tell she'd been sleeping by the way she snuggled into Marissa's neck. Watching them together took his breath away. How many times had he dreamt of this very scene as he'd lie awake in his bunk at the academy missing Marissa? Too many to count he admitted to himself. He walked toward them and was pleased to see a look of relief on Marissa's face when she spotted him.

"I'm so glad you're here," she whispered, trying not to disturb Chloe. "It's nice to see a friendly face. California drivers..." she trailed off with a shrug of her shoulders.

"I'm glad you're home in one piece." He lifted the bag she'd set on the ground and followed her inside. Realizing he'd left the television on and not exactly at a low volume, he rushed to shut it off as Marissa gently laid Chloe against the cushions on the couch and covered her with a throw blanket.

Jordan studied the sleeping girl and Marissa's natural way with her. He knew from the day he'd met her she'd make a great mother. He also knew how badly she'd wanted it. There was a small part of him selfishly grateful she didn't have any children with Steven after the man had broken her heart.

Chloe whimpered and shifted her position, giving Jordan a better look at her. She reminded him of a thin cherub with pink cheeks and red lips puckered like she was waiting for a kiss. In her tiny arms she held a stuffed ladybug, an obvious gift from Marissa.

"How are you holding up?"

"I'm exhausted, hungry, and completely out of my mind. She's so small, so fragile, so innocent. What if one day she figures out who I really am? I don't even want to think about how she'll feel if she learns the truth."

He'd had enough of this self-doubt from her. "First of all, you are the most incredible woman I've ever known, and she is lucky fate brought her here, to be with you. Two, you're racing ahead of yourself. It'll be your story to tell her when the time comes and in any way you choose." He reached down and squeezed her shoulders gently, fighting an old urge to run his fingers through her hair. "I made dinner, are you ready to eat?"

"Do I smell spaghetti?" She smiled and this one reached her eyes. "You're too good to me."

"It was for Chloe, but I figured there was enough for you, too." He laughed as she playfully slapped him on the arm. "Let me help you get the car unloaded and then I'll feed you."

A flash of panic crossed her face as she looked over at Chloe, still sleeping on the couch. She pulled the coffee table back, and laid a stack of pillows on the floor before placing one directly in front of the child on the couch. "Will she be okay? Should I stay with her?" Her bright, amber eyes were filled with worry.

"She'll be fine, I promise," he reassured her. "I'll unpack the car while you watch her, then we'll wake her up for dinner. How does that sound?"

He smiled at the grateful look on her face and the rapid nod of her head.

By the time he'd emptied the trunk he wondered how anyone could afford to have a child. Did they really need all of this stuff? He finished just in time to watch as Marissa gently woke Chloe. He was surprised to see the immediate recognition on the little girl's face and the easy way she lifted her arms to Marissa. It hadn't taken Chloe long to fall in love with her new mom.

He set up the high chair while Marissa set the table. Like he'd been doing it for years, he cut up Chloe's spaghetti into a bowl and set it aside to cool while he dished up their plates and placed the salad and bread onto the table. Marissa poured the wine and pulled a sipper cup from one of the bags he'd carried in and filled it with milk.

This was the kind of life he'd always wanted. Marissa moaned with pleasure as she chewed, and watching her intently, Chloe dug her spoon in and took a bite as well.

After dinner, Jordan volunteered to clean the kitchen while she gave Chloe a bath. After he'd turned on the dishwasher, he climbed the stairs and stood outside the bathroom in silence, watching the two of them. Chloe didn't smile, but her eyes never left Marissa's face. With her remarkable resemblance to Steven, he could only imagine what Marissa's reaction must have been when she'd seen Chloe.

She lifted Chloe from the tub and he handed her a towel. He stepped back to watch as Marissa dressed her and combed her hair. Marissa stood and held out her hand—instead Chloe held up her arms to be carried.

"Poor baby's been through a lot the last few weeks," he said, thinking aloud.

By the time she'd put Chloe to bed fifteen minutes later, Jordan had made his way back downstairs and topped off their wine glasses.

"She went right out," Marissa told him with a tired smile of her own. "She's beautiful, isn't she?"

He patted the couch for her to join him. "She is."

She settled onto the couch beside him and kicked her feet beneath her. "It's strange, isn't it, my suddenly having a child. Giving her baths, cutting spaghetti, tucking her in."

"You're a natural with her."

She smiled, seeming pleased with the reassurance.

"How'd it all go?"

"It went okay." She sipped from her glass. "I had to go to Steven and Jane's place to get some of Chloe's things."

Damn. He'd have definitely gone with her if he'd known she'd be asked to do something so painful. "I'm sorry, that couldn't have been easy."

"It was so cold."

"What was cold?" he asked.

"Their house. It surprised me how different it was from ours…I mean mine." She sighed. "The only room with any life was Chloe's. The rest of the house was black, glass, cold, like a showroom."

Jordan let her talk, fighting to keep the anger he felt from showing. How could Steven have been so selfish, so insensitive? How could he not know how lucky he was to have a woman like Marissa in his life?

"He took his parents' photo to his house with her."

Jordan knit his brow in confusion.

"The only photo he had left of his parents. It was his prized possession. I found it sitting on the dresser in their bedroom."

"You went into their bedroom?" he blurted. Why would she do that? It was like asking to be hurt, asking to have the wounds opened wider. It didn't make sense.

Her cheeks grew red. "I couldn't help it. It was like my legs had a mind of their own."

"Ouch," he mumbled.

She turned to him, her intensity surprising him. "How long have I been a fool? How long had he lived with her and I kept patiently waiting for him to drop by? Did he just slowly start moving his things in with her and I never noticed? Was I that stupid to not see what was going on?"

Jordan ran his hand through his hair and felt himself begin to sweat. He'd never seen her look the way she did. It was like she really expected him to answer her, and he wished more than anything he could. Without thought, he reached up his hand again, and jerked it down to his lap. The last thing he needed right now was for Marissa to notice his nerves. What she deserved were answers to her questions, but he knew the answers he could give her would only lead to more questions.

"You weren't a fool, Marissa, nor are you stupid. You were deceived. It's not fair, but it's not your fault."

Her eyes begged for understanding, but it was her lips he couldn't tear his gaze from. Every part of her was vulnerable, and every part of him knew he had no right, but he bent down and pressed his lips to hers anyway. It felt familiar, but different, and he didn't want it to stop.

A terrified scream shot through the room, and both of them jumped from the couch. Jordan felt a moment of panic, then shame when Marissa looked at him with confused eyes.

"It's Chloe," she said bolting for the stairs.

"You take care of her, I'll let myself out. Welcome to motherhood," he managed, trying to lighten the moment yet unable to meet her gaze.

He watched her race upstairs and quietly locked the door behind him.

Chapter 7

It felt good to be back at work. She was grateful for the distraction and her familiar routine. Working at the Nathan Talbot Hospice House wasn't a job most people could handle. In the three weeks she'd been gone, Mr. Preston, a professor at the local university, had passed away from pancreatic cancer at age fifty-eight, and Lucas, a twenty-three-year-old aspiring meteorologist, lost his fight with liver cancer.

It was a sad reality dealing with death every day, but Marissa was happy knowing she brought her patients comfort in their final hours.

She smiled as she opened the last door in the hallway. Annie was one of her favorite patients. At seventy-four she had more spunk than most young, healthy people, and her outlook was inspiring. She'd fought her lymphoma with everything she had, but the cancer was stronger than her will. She'd finally stopped her treatments in order to enjoy her final months without the side effects she'd endured for so long. She still had pain, but they'd been able to manage it without having her sleep through the day, which had been her only request.

"Marissa, there you are," Annie sang. "I was afraid I'd missed you during my cat nap."

Annie didn't have anyone to visit her. She'd lost her husband eight years earlier and they'd never been able to have children. If Marissa was all this woman had, she would be there for her.

"You know I would have woken you—I selfishly can't get through my day without seeing your smiling face." Marissa sat beside her bed. "How are you feeling?"

"I'm feeling fine; ready to go out dancing if I could talk my favorite nurse into breaking me out of this joint." Annie chuckled, her voice weak but her eyes full of laughter.

"I couldn't possibly go dancing with you, Annie; you'd wear me out, show me up, and steal all the boys."

She laughed again and squeezed Marissa's hand. "You rascal, you always know what to say to make this old gal's day."

Marissa creased her brow and looked around the room. "Old gal—who are you talking about?"

"Aw, you..." Annie blushed, the pink color a beautiful change from the pale, gray pallor. Her hair had also started to grow back, tufts of white curls springing up sparsely.

Marissa ran a soft brush through Annie's hair and listened as she reminisced about the years her young husband had taken her out to the dance halls, and how the music had been upbeat and lively. "Nothing like this nonsense they call music now." Annie crinkled her nose in disapproval.

Sitting on the edge of her bed, they chatted for a while about everything from knitting and recipes to the feel of the sun on your face and sand in your toes.

Annie's eyes grew serious, and she reached out and grasped Marissa's hand. "I'm sorry about your loss, and the hurt you must be feeling."

Marissa nodded her head.

"We're friends, you and I, and more; you are the daughter I never had."

Her throat clogged with emotion. Unable to speak, she squeezed Annie's hand.

"I know you can't see it now, but this is a blessing. You were not destined to be with Steven. Not like me and my Charlie. Your destiny is waiting for you. So forgive quickly, let your anger go, and embrace the path you're on now. Life is too short, and each moment should be cherished like it's the last." Annie closed her eyes for a minute, and Marissa reached for the glass of water on the table and held the straw to the woman's lips. Her eyes lit up gratefully as she took a small sip. "And you are going to be a wonderful mother. Chloe is lucky to have you. I knew she would come to you."

"What do you mean, you knew she would come?"

"I saw her in a dream." Annie closed her eyes again, her voice barely a whisper. "Don't be afraid, Marissa. She was always yours. And she needs you desperately."

Marissa had so many questions, but they would have to wait. Annie had fallen asleep. With a final check of the machine beside her bed, Marissa quietly let herself out.

Chapter 8

"He what?" Lexie slapped her thigh and let out a whoop. "It's about time."

Crap. Why had she thought it would be a good idea to tell Lexie that Jordan had kissed her? "It's not funny, Lex. I don't want his pity."

The business phone rang and Lexie held up a finger before answering it. It was nice working with her best friend, but it also made it overly convenient to share things she regretted the moment they left her lips.

The moment she'd hung up the phone, her voice rose, "Are you kidding me?" With a quick look around the silent reception area, she lowered it to a whisper. "You know it's not pity, Marissa. You may be hurt, but you didn't suddenly become stupid."

"Okay, Lex, don't hold back, tell me how you really feel." Marissa picked up a chart and pretended to study it. She should have known Lexie wouldn't understand. She may be her best friend, but since the day Marissa married Steven, Lexie made it clear she thought it was a mistake. Lexie always believed she was meant to be with Jordan. But what else should she expect when Jordan was her brother?

She hadn't heard from Jordan in a week. She tried to convince herself he wasn't avoiding her but simply respecting her time of adjustment with Chloe.

If the truth were told, she'd enjoyed his kiss, and she yearned for it to happen again. The scene played repetitively in her mind. It had felt so natural; so right. She sighed. How would she know what was right? Wasn't she the one running back to her high school sweetheart like it could somehow change the outcome of the years she'd been betrayed by Steven?

She hadn't realized how lost in her thoughts she was until Lexie rose and began staring at her, forcing her to look up. When their eyes met, she said, "I'm sorry Steven hurt you. I'm sorry he didn't appreciate the great woman you are. But your life isn't over, Marissa. You need to grasp whatever happiness you can." She motioned her arm across the room of the hospice. "You and I know better than anyone."

Marissa rose and wrapped her arms around her friend. "You're right," she said. "And after that painful admission, I'm going to change the subject."

Lexie chuckled.

"How are you feeling?"

Lexie rubbed her pregnant belly proudly. "I'm doing great. I feel energized, and I love being pregnant." She smiled softly, her face glowing, and Marissa could feel the happiness radiating from her.

"I need to get on my rounds, but I'm so happy for you. Who would've thought we'd be here, you having a baby and me raising a beautiful little girl?"

"Me." Lexie smirked.

Throughout the rest of her shift, Marissa was surprised how much she missed Chloe. Although grateful that Jordan's mother, Betty, had leapt at the chance to watch her while she worked, she couldn't help but wish they were together. On this first day back, she found herself constantly looking at her watch, praying it was four o'clock.

Chloe had settled in to their new routine better than she'd expected. After the third night of her waking up screaming in terror, Marissa finally realized she was scared to death of the dark. She'd picked up a cute night light that projected pink butterflies across the ceiling, and since then, both of them slept peacefully.

Chloe still wouldn't talk, however, and refused to potty train. Although Marissa was worried about the setbacks, she also understood there was no way of knowing how the trauma of losing her parents would affect Chloe.

Heading back to the reception area, Marissa could hear Lexie's son, Ryan, giggling the moment she entered. He ran at her full speed and threw himself into her arms, knocking her backward. "Aunty Rissa," he sang, "I missed you, how come you don't come to my beach no more?"

She squeezed him and kissed his cheeks until he begged for release. "I've been busy, but I promise Chloe and I will make it out to your beach very soon," she told him, setting him back on the ground.

He puffed his chest out and stood as tall as his little four-year-old legs could stretch. "I'm awesome on the board now. I can even stand without help. Pretty soon I'll be able to ride me a wave," he bragged.

"I can't wait to see that," she told him. "You're growing up so fast."

Ryan nodded his head vigorously, "Yep, I am."

Looking around, Marissa waved at Betty, who also watched her grandson when Lexie was on shift.

"Ryan, where is Chloe?"

He shrugged his shoulders and raced toward the desk chair, plopped into the seat, and began to spin.

Marissa scanned the reception area. "Chloe?" Marissa called out. "Chloe, come here, sweetie." Her heart began to beat faster, and her voice rose as she began to panic. "Chloe?"

She poked her head into the child's playhouse in the corner, checked the bathrooms, and rushed out the front doors, looking both ways for any sign of her daughter. Nothing.

Back in the reception area, Betty and Lexie were searching as well. Marissa could see Betty's eyes filled with tears. "It's not your fault, Betty, she's here somewhere," she soothed, trying desperately to convince herself at the same time.

Frantic now, Marissa began to go door to door down the hall, her palms sweaty and the tears flowing unchecked down her cheeks. She continued to call Chloe's name, even when she doubted the girl would respond. She was about to phone the police when she heard voices coming from behind Annie's door. Marissa froze at the sound of a toddler's tinkling laughter.

Opening the door slowly, she poked her head in, hoping to remain undetected. Her breath hitched at the scene. Chloe had climbed up from the chair onto Annie's bed and was giggling as the old woman sang *Itsy Bitsy Spider* and inched her fingers up Chloe's arm. Annie's face beamed, her cheeks flushed, and Chloe's happiness was contagious.

Struggling to shut down her practical side and ignore the flash of disaster that crossed her mind—Chloe falling off the bed, the chair flipping when she'd climbed up on it, or bumping one of Annie's IV lines, for starters—Marissa focused on the delight shining on both of their faces and the heartwarming sound of Chloe's voice.

With a smile on her face, she walked into the room. "There you are, Chloe." She ran her hand gently across the cherub face. "You scared the life out of me."

"Oh Marissa, she's such a sweet girl," Annie said, reaching in to tickle Chloe on her tummy.

Chloe grinned and arched her back in reaction to being tickled, but this time there was no sound.

"I've never heard her laugh make a sound before," she told Annie. "It gives me hope to hear it now."

"Hope for what, dear?"

Marissa looked at Chloe intently. "Hope that she'll be happy, that she'll laugh and play like a normal two-year-old." She lowered her voice to a whisper, "Hope that she'll be happy with me."

"She isn't a normal two-year-old, she's special, and she is happy with you." Annie smiled. "You can't see it yet because of your own unhappiness and insecurities, but you will."

Marissa creased her brow and stared doubtfully at the pair. "I appreciate your confidence."

Annie reached out and laid her hand over Marissa's and squeezed gently, her eyes growing serious. "She was meant to be with you, Marissa."

"I love her very much."

"Hold tightly to that," Annie whispered as her eyes began to close. She was asleep in seconds.

Chapter 9

With the back of his hand, Jordan wiped the sweat from his brow and lifted the grass bagger to empty. Marissa's once pristine lawn was now four inches high, and her flowerbeds were more weeds then flowers. He realized he was going to have to mow it twice. He'd tried desperately to keep his distance from Marissa. He wasn't sure he was comfortable with the feelings that were stirring in him when he thought of her. *You're an idiot, Jordan Wayne,* he thought to himself as he started the mower again. He was playing house with a woman who'd once broken his heart and still hadn't recovered from the pain her deceased husband caused.

He wanted to finish the back yard and have time to put up the swing set he'd purchased for Chloe. In no time, that little angel had wrapped herself around his heart.

Intent on his task, he jumped when Marissa shouted his name over the sound of the mower. Releasing the handle, he smiled when she handed him a cold beer.

"You didn't have to mow my lawn, Jordan. I would have gotten to it, or hired someone to get to it for me," she said, but her eyes showed appreciation.

"It's no problem. I don't get to do this stuff at my condo and I kind of enjoy it. Besides, I came across a swing set I wanted to put up for Chloe." He took a large pull from his cold beer.

She laughed. "Came across?"

He shrugged his shoulders casually. He felt a tug on his pant leg and his heart swelled when he looked down to see Chloe holding her arms up. Without a thought to his currently filthy condition, he lifted her and kissed her cheek. "Hello, beautiful." He snuggled into her neck and blew, creating a vibration that made her tilt her head against his, a huge grin on her face.

Marissa took Chloe from his arms. "We're going to start dinner. Plan on staying—it's the least we can do to repay you for the yard work." She looked over her shoulder as she walked toward the house, and smirked. "And, of course, for coming across an abandoned swing set still in the box."

He laughed and started the mower again.

Later, after multiple bruises, curse words, and a few splinters, he stood back, placed his hands on his hips, and admired the play set he'd finally put together.

"Nice work," Marissa said, walking up beside him.

"Piece of cake," he said, tucking his beaten hands into his pockets.

It was obvious by her laughter she'd witnessed his fight with each piece. Pretending to ignore her, he grunted and reached over to take Chloe out of her arms. He placed her into the tot seat and gently pushed her back to let her swing. A brief moment of panic flashed across Chloe's face, followed by a huge grin. She kicked her feet in excitement when Jordan pushed her again, this time letting the swing go a little higher and faster.

"She loves it," Marissa said. "Thank you, Jordan. This was so thoughtful of you." She laid her head briefly on his collarbone, and he reached his arm around her shoulder, tucking her against his side.

He wondered if she could remember as vividly as he did the night they'd spent together before she left for college. The night they lost their virginity to each other, the soft light of the moon shining down on them as they discovered how to please each other, and how right it felt to lie together; naked and satisfied.

He shook his head to scatter his thoughts. It was ancient history now. "Do you mind if I take a quick shower before dinner?" he asked, pulling quickly away from her.

"Sure, it'll be ready in twenty minutes or so," she told him, reaching out to push Chloe on the swing again.

After a cold shower and a firm lecture to himself, he strolled into the kitchen and took the open seat across from her. The urge to kiss her was strong, but after the look on her face the last time he'd tasted her lips, he decided against repeating it.

Over baked chicken and mashed potatoes, they chatted like an old married couple about Chloe's adventure at the hospice, and her attachment to Marissa's favorite patient, Annie. The sound of Marissa's voice made his blood heat and his heart race. Her tone was deep, yet feminine and sexy. She had the kind of voice that made people want to listen, regardless of what she was saying. Her laugh was musical, contagious, and a sound he'd missed more than he'd realized. He was starting to feel like the teenage boy he used to be when he was around her.

He helped with the dishes, and they laughed as they discussed their upcoming ten year high school reunion being held on a dinner cruise ship. He wondered how different their reunion would be if they were actually married. Would their old classmates be awed that they were still together, and wish they had a love like theirs? Would they walk along the beach and kiss under the stars after the boat returned to the docks? Would they plan a night away and check into a hotel on the water for a night alone?

"I'm taking Lexie as my date," she snickered, sliding a plate into the dishwasher. "If nothing else, she'll make sure it's not boring."

Guess that made it clear where he stood. Why did he suddenly feel rejected? Had he wondered if they would actually attend the reunion together now that Steven was gone? He sighed as he realized that was exactly what he'd thought. After wiping down the counters, placing the crystal bowl back as the centerpiece on the table, and tucking Chloe's highchair back into the corner, he hung up the towel and started for the door. "I'm going to head out."

Marissa looked surprised. "Already? I thought maybe we could watch a movie or something after I tuck Chloe in."

Of course she did, he thought to himself. Her good ole' friend Jordan never had plans that didn't revolve around her. Maybe it was time he started exploring a new relationship between them.

He watched her amber eyes flash with confusion as he took a step toward her. She attempted to retreat, but he grasped her around the waist and pulled her to him more roughly than he intended. Her body pressed to his, and her mouth opened in shock when he lowered his head and devoured her mouth with his. Raising his hands he slid them into her soft, auburn hair, and kissed her even deeper.

Abruptly, he stepped back and let his arms fall to his side. Marissa stood there, slightly rocking back and forth, her lips red, her eyes cloudy.

He walked over and ruffled Chloe's hair, before turning back to Marissa. "Good night, thank you for dinner."

He walked away, satisfied by the puzzled look on her face. *Maybe she'll think of her good ole' friend Jordan a little differently now*, he thought as he closed the door tightly behind him.

Chapter 10

Marissa sat beside Lexie on the patio and watched as Chloe and Ryan blew bubbles in the backyard. She was surprised how patient Lexie's son was with Chloe. Even when she spilled her bubbles into the grass, he simply handed her his bottle.

She sipped her lemonade and kicked her shoes off, pulling her legs beneath her on the bench. "Ryan is going to be such a great big brother."

Lexie smiled. "He's so excited."

Chloe giggled when a bubble she blew popped on Ryan's nose. Marissa's heart swelled at the sound. She'd never imagined how wonderful it could feel to have Chloe in her life. For the first time in as long as she could remember, she felt complete. Even when she had the occasional bouts of loneliness, she was happy with her life now.

Although she couldn't deny how much she'd missed Jordan lately.

It'd been eleven days since she'd seen or heard from him. Eleven days since he'd left her standing in her kitchen struggling for breath after he'd kissed her so thoroughly she'd actually felt the air drift from her lungs. He'd learned a few things since the summer after high school.

Why had he kissed her? And why was he now avoiding her? It wasn't as if he refused to answer her calls—she hadn't tried to call him—but still, it was unusual for him not to drop by every few days, and this was the second time he'd stayed away.

"What are you thinking about so seriously?" Lexie interrupted her thoughts.

She sighed. "Honestly, your brother. I haven't heard from him in almost two weeks."

Lexie scrunched her brow. "That's not like him."

"I don't know why he hasn't come by, or even called."

"Did you two get into an argument?"

Marissa shook her head. "He hasn't said anything, has he?"

"Not a word. In fact, now that you mention it, I haven't really seen him either. Maybe he's met a hot woman and he can't climb out of bed." She chuckled.

Marissa felt a sharp pain in her chest, and the air rushed from her lungs like she'd been punched.

"Oh my God," Lexie shouted. "You're as white as a sheet. Something's going on between you and Jordan. Spill it."

"Nothing's going on," Marissa stammered. "Not really."

"What's 'not really?'"

Marissa could feel the heat creep into her cheeks. "I don't know…it's nothing…I just…well…"

"You just what?"

"After he kissed me again—"

"He kissed you *again*?" Lexie's eyes grew large.

She nodded her head. "And it was hot…and sudden…and… and I haven't been able to think of much else since it happened." She exhaled a deep breath. "It's crazy, right? I mean he's my friend, and what we had together was ten years ago."

"Why would that matter?" Lexie asked.

"Because, we were kids. I hurt him and married Steven, and we are friends."

She knew she was talking in circles, but she couldn't figure out how to put her thoughts into words, or how to make her friend understand when she didn't either.

"Have you asked yourself why he kissed you if he only sees you as a friend?" Lexie's expression made her feel like a fool.

"No…yes…but…"

"Marissa," Lexie sighed. "If you want him, do something about it. Don't sit around and wait for him to come to you. I may be prejudiced, as he is my brother, but you'd be a fool to let him slip away."

She was starting to believe the same thing.

Chapter 11

Marissa stood in the mirror and turned slowly in a circle. The red dress she'd chosen was exactly what she'd been looking for. It accentuated her curves, enhanced the strawberry highlights in her hair, and made her amber eyes bright. After eighteen days without a word from Jordan, she'd made her decision, and tonight she planned on making him remember what they used to have together.

Chloe sat at her feet, running her small fingers over the strappy black heels she wore. "What do you think, Chloe?" she asked smiling down at her cherub face.

The doorbell rang, and despite the chance of her dress wrinkling, she carried Chloe down the stairs. She opened the door for Betty, who'd volunteered to babysit. After her normal tickle greetings with Chloe, she noticed Marissa and let out a soft whistle. She took the baby and instructed Marissa to spin.

"I have a feeling I'll be getting a call from the hospital tonight. Jordan is going to have a heart attack when he sees you in that dress. Marissa, you're stunning."

She couldn't help but smile. She couldn't remember the last time someone had given her a compliment. With Steven she'd always felt invisible. "I'm going to the reunion with Lexie," she corrected.

"That is just a small detail. You didn't wear that dress for Lexie." Betty smiled slyly and handed Marissa her purse. "Have fun, and don't worry about Chloe and I. We will be fine." She winked at her. "Now scoot, have a wonderful time."

•••

Marissa's stomach began to flutter with every step she took closer to the ship hosting their ten-year high school reunion, ironically named *Destiny*.

Jordan had been a part of her life for as long as she could remember, so why was she so anxious she felt her legs might crumble beneath her at any minute? She needed to pull it together.

Lexie patted her arm in reassurance. "It's going to be fine."

If she only knew what was going through her mind, Lexie would be running for the ship, dragging Marissa behind her. She hadn't realized she'd chuckled aloud until Lexie asked, "What's so funny?"

She insisted it was nothing but her nerves, and slowly made her way up the ramp and into the crowd. It wasn't a surprise how many people knew Lexie, but she was surprised how many people knew about Steven's death. Each greeting was "I'm so sorry for your loss," and "Wow, you look amazing." For the widow of a cheating bastard, she supposed she did.

Although Marissa tried to stay focused on each person she stopped to speak with, she continued to scan the crowds for Jordan. Now that she'd made up her mind, she was in a rush to find him before she lost her nerve.

She finally made it inside and through the long line at the open bar. Drink in hand, she stood beside Lexie at the side of the large open room, sipping her wine and watching the people enter.

"I wonder if Willow Southland will rise from the pits of hell for the reunion," Lexie said, scrunching her nose.

Marissa laughed. That was the one piece of history she'd prefer not to relive tonight. "I'm not sure that would be a wise decision. I can count at least twenty people who would love to throw her overboard if she did show."

"And the first one in line would be you." Lexie nudged her with her elbow.

Marissa lifted her hand to her chest in astonishment. "I would never stoop so low as to toss someone overboard." Unable to keep up the pretense, she laughed. "Unless it was Willow Southland. That girl made my life hell in high school."

"She sure hated you," Lexie agreed.

"Do you remember that stunt she pulled my senior year?"

Lexie looked up toward the ceiling, as if searching for the correct answer. "Which stunt was that? There were so many to choose from."

"I was referring to the time she wrote that note to Jordan, claiming it was from me."

"The one where you told him you were breaking up with him because *you* suddenly fell in love with what's his name?"

"John Patson," Marissa remembered.

"He crushed on you all through high school, poor guy. He never stood a chance."

She grimaced. "And she'd sent John a note supposedly from me begging him to take me to prom."

"That's right! He started bragging that you were his girl and Jordan lost it and punched him."

"Broke his nose," she smirked.

"Willow was something else." Lexie shook her head. "She sure wanted my brother and hated you because he didn't want her. Speaking of my brother, have you seen him?"

"I haven't, but he'll find us," she replied, willing it to be.

Lexie covered her mouth to stifle a laugh. "*Now* this is funny."

Marissa followed her gaze. John Patson was walking toward them.

"He certainly grew up nice," her friend whispered out of the corner of her mouth. "He is *hot*."

Marissa had to agree, he did look good; he always had. But the truth was in high school she'd had eyes only for Jordan. "Hi John, it's nice to see you."

"Marissa, you look beautiful." He turned to Lexie. "You're Jordan Wayne's sister…Alexis, right?"

"Lexie, yes." Lexie took his outstretched hand, her eyes gleaming mischievously.

John's friendly smile faded, and he glared over her shoulder. "Marissa, I hope to see you again. Now, if you two will excuse me." His unease was apparent as he walked away.

Turning around to see what had caused his sudden departure, Lexie grunted. "Well there goes a nice evening."

Marissa turned and locked eyes with Willow Southland.

"Willow, how nice to see you," she lied. "You look amazing." Much to her disgust, that part was true. Her long, blonde hair fell in a silky sheet, and with her blue eyes, pouty mouth, and perfect nose, she was the woman other women stopped and stared at. Since high school, she'd purchased breasts that rose perfectly out of a black sequined dress and balanced a large diamond hanging from a chain.

Lexie crinkled her nose and asked, "Is the nose new, too, or just the boobs?"

Willow's smile was wily. "Oh, Lexie, it's so nice to see you haven't changed a bit; still the same ill-mannered girl, only now you've obviously found a nice blind and deaf man to care for you, congratulations," She said sweetly, staring at Lexie's protruding stomach. Willow turned her attention to Marissa. "I was sorry to hear about Steven. Not surprised really, but I can imagine you were. You always were one to see the good in everyone. Or maybe it was your simple nature blinding you from the signs in front of you. Either way, it must be difficult knowing your husband had another family and chose them over you. You poor thing, I can't even imagine."

Marissa clenched her fingers tightly around the clasp of her bag, willing herself to keep her hands from flying around Willow's neck.

Lexie clucked her tongue. "And I understand you've never been married. Is your dowry really so small, your father hasn't been able to purchase you a husband yet?"

The blonde began to reply, her face growing red with anger, but she suddenly stopped, smiled smugly, and said, "I was simply waiting for the one I wanted to come to his senses. I'm happy to say that after a long, sizzling two weeks, he has."

Marissa's head jerked up when Jordan approached them and handed Willow a glass of wine. "Sorry it took so long; the line is wrapped around the room."

Willow wrapped her arms around Jordan's waist. "You were worth waiting for," she purred.

Marissa's heart lurched.

"What in the…" Lexie's face turned crimson as she balled her fists. She took a step forward, appearing ready to physically rip the two of them apart. The veins in her neck pulsed, her mouth pressed into a straight line, and her eyes shot daggers at her brother. Marissa grabbed hold of her arm in an attempt to stop any bloodshed. "Are you kidding me?" Lexie spat.

Ignoring Lexie, Jordan locked eyes with Marissa, his eyes scanning her from head to toe.

This was the scene she'd imagined. He stood there, dressed to kill in a dark suit accentuating his broad shoulders, a red tie that matched her dress, his hair thick and begging to have her hands run through it. His eyes swept over her like a caress, and she would step toward him and place her lips to his ear and tell him the things she'd like to do to him after the ship docked.

What she hadn't envisioned was the slap of reality when instead Willow reached up and pressed her lips to his.

Marissa swallowed hard and excused herself. Grabbing Lexie's hand, she dragged her through the crowd. She needed off this boat. Lexie was still cursing Jordan and inventing ways to dismember Willow when they finally made it through the crowds to the deck.

Marissa's heart sank when she watched the ramp pull back and the horn sound as the ship pulled away from the dock, trapping her onboard with Jordan—and Willow.

Chapter 12

She walked back into the main room of the ship where the lights were dimmed and the music and dancing started. Marissa choked back a sob as she watched Jordan hold tightly to Willow, swaying as one body to the song the band was playing.

Lexie's eyes filled with sympathy, but her jaw set in anger. "Wait here," she instructed.

She watched Lexie wobble over to the bar, and leaning over the counter as far as her belly would allow, she boldly flirted with the good-looking bartender. Both of them pointed at her, and the bartender mouthed "I'm so sorry."

With a triumphant grin, Lexie walked back, grabbed her hand, and pulled her from the room. Continuing to drag Marissa behind her, Lexie walked along the deck.

"Where are we going?" Marissa asked impatiently as the cold wind blasted through her thin dress.

"Just trust me," Lexie replied, finally stopping and opening a door with "Employees Only" painted in bright red letters.

"Trust you?" Marissa bit back. "You pulled me into an area we shouldn't be in. It was *very* clearly marked."

Lexie tossed her head back and laughed, the sound bouncing off the steel walls surrounding them. "Lighten up, Marissa, we're reminiscing our old high school days, aren't we?"

"How is this reminiscing our high school days?"

"I keep forgetting what a goody-two-shoes you were." Lexie shook her head. "No wonder we weren't best friends until after you returned from college. Boor-ring."

"I wasn't boring," Marissa pouted. "I was well behaved."

"Same thing." Lexie stopped, looked up and down the hallway, and slipped inside a door off the engine room, closing it tightly behind them.

Lexie sat cross-legged on the floor, motioning for Marissa to sit beside her, and pulled out a full bottle of tequila. "Compliments of the hot bartender," she said with a wink.

This wasn't good. Marissa didn't drink. Well, wine didn't count. Yet here she was; cross legged on the floor of a supply closet they weren't supposed to be in, beside her enabling best friend who was determined to get her drunk while she watched. She scrunched her nose at the smell before tossing back the shot Lexie handed her. Goosebumps popped up on her arms and she struggled to keep the foul liquid down.

Lexie laughed at her. "You really are a goody-two-shoes, aren't you?"

She scowled. "Am not," she said childishly, while taking the shot glass from her and drinking again. The liquid warmed a path down her chest, and Marissa began to relax. "Can you believe Jordan had the audacity to bring Willow as his date?"

"I wouldn't call it audacity," Lexie huffed. "I'd call it a death wish."

Marissa drank another and hiccupped. "I wish she wasn't so stinking beautiful."

Lexie whipped her head around like she'd been slapped. "Beautiful?" she barked. "You think that phony, plastic Barbie doll with the fake hair extensions, glued on eyelashes, and body by Doctor Sven is beautiful?"

She nodded her head. "Yep." She blinked, trying to focus on Lexie. Her friend was blurry, but as she came into focus, there was no missing the disgusted look on her face. "But I still hate her," she said matter-of-factly tossing back another shot.

"Why does Jordan like her?" She reached for the glass only to have Lexie slap her hand away.

"Jordan doesn't like her," her friend snapped. "He's blinded by her rock hard boobs and megawatt smile."

"I want rock hard boobs," she whined. "I want Jordan to like me more."

"Willow is no competition, Marissa. Jordan isn't stupid. He's a man, plain and simple."

"But I wanted him to want me," she huffed. "Not her. Never her."

Marissa felt a sudden urge to cry. She wanted to be dancing with Jordan, feeling his arms around her, looking into his beautiful eyes, and feeling him against her. She didn't want him with Willow. She closed her eyes for a moment, and instantly regretted it when the dizzy feeling intensified.

"It's just poor timing," her friend reassured. "You will just have to make it clear to him what you want."

Marissa gasped. "You mean, like just say it?"

Lexie roared with laughter, and Marissa covered her ears at the shattering sound. Seconds later, the door flew open and two men dressed in sailor uniforms walked in.

"Crap," Lexie whispered as she stood up and reached down to help her.

Marissa found it impossible to stand. The ship rocked so hard she was surprised Lexie and the sailors were able to stay on their feet. She batted away Lexie's outstretched hand. "I'm staying here."

"I'm sorry ma'am, but we're going to have to ask you to leave," one of the guys in white said.

She heard Lexie speak but couldn't make out what she said. Marissa lay down on the floor, letting the waves rock her. She decided she'd let Lexie convince the sailor men she didn't want to leave yet.

Chapter 13

Damn her! Jordan plopped onto his bed, kicked off his shoes, and loosened his tie. Why, when a beautiful woman like Willow Southland slid off her dress and stood before him in a sexy black bra and panties, did he automatically wish it was Marissa? Why did the black dress that hit the floor suddenly become red silk, and the eyes begging him to kiss her appear amber instead of blue?

He wasn't sure who he was angriest at, Marissa or himself. Deep down he knew he'd agreed to go with Willow to get a reaction from her. They'd been out a few times over the years, and he'd never seen the side of her his sister and Marissa claimed to see, but as much as he enjoyed her company upon occasion, he wasn't interested. She was beautiful, and easy to talk to, but also shallow and needy. He'd never been drawn to her the way most men would be. Then again, he never was one to be attracted to looks over substance.

After he'd kissed Marissa, he'd stayed away, secretly hoping she'd call, show up, kiss him, tell him she was attracted to him the way he was for her. It hadn't happened, and once he'd realized she wasn't feeling what he was, he'd accepted Willow's invitation.

He threw his shirt onto the chair, took off his belt, and headed to the bathroom to take a cold shower. Sadly, he wondered if instead of making her jealous, he'd actually hurt her. That wasn't what he'd intended, and he hadn't seen Lexie or Marissa after the ship left the dock. He almost wondered if they'd disembarked, which was probably best for his safety. Lexie obviously wanted to choke the life from him when she realized he'd brought Willow.

Reaching down to turn on the water, he was surprised to hear his doorbell. He flipped the water off and wrapped a towel around his waist. He hitched a breath when he opened the door and found Marissa grasping tightly to the doorframe.

She stumbled and he reached out to balance her. She was drunk. Completely annihilated, down to her wide eyes and slurred speech. She was in the red dress she'd worn, one shoe off and dangling from her finger. She bent over, trying to remove the other shoe but kept tumbling backward. The man beside her wore an apologetic expression as he propped her up each time she leaned back.

"I didn't want to just let her out without making sure she got inside," he said sheepishly. "I think she's had a bit to drink."

Jordan thanked the cab driver and tried to help Marissa inside. Finally slipping her shoe off her foot, she tossed it inside and reached forward, running her hand down his chest. "Mmm," she hummed, stepping closer to him. In all his fantasies lately, never had he imagined she'd smell like tequila.

She walked past him, swaying from side to side. "Willow?" she called out. "Get out here, not gonna be so easy now. I'm...I'm... pushing baaack."

Jordan shook his head as he watched her lean on the arm of the couch to keep herself from falling. "Marissa, Willow isn't here."

"Nooo?" she slurred, turning around a little too fast and grasping onto the couch again. "She's gone?" Even trying to be... well, whatever she was trying to be, he could see the flash of relief in her currently bloodshot eyes.

She stepped toward him, struggling to keep her eyes focused on his. "I want you," she told him, reaching her hand out to touch him, obviously not realizing she was still so far away. He took a step forward to cut that distance for her.

She fell forward, her hands flailing as she searched for something to stop her fall. She grabbed at the only thing in front of her, and toppled over, taking his towel with her.

Jordan knew that tomorrow he would find this scene extremely entertaining. But now, standing in front of her naked while she lay at his feet, he didn't. Reaching down he tried to pull the towel from her grip, but she pulled it against her chest and, propping up on her arms, smiled at him.

"You…you want me," she said, trying to pull herself up from the floor.

"Marissa, hand me my towel." His voice was stern, but she didn't seem to believe him.

Now on her feet, she waved it back and forth. "Nope, not—" she hiccupped, "happening." She plopped down on the couch and buried her head into the towel on her lap. "I don't feel so good."

Still naked, he picked her up and carried her through his room, heading for the bathroom. She snuggled into his neck, her breathing hard. "You smell good." Her head fell back, her hair brushing against his arm as her head lolled from side to side.

He could tell by the change in her breathing she was going to be sick. He hurried his pace and gently set her onto the floor by the toilet and lifted the lid. She emptied her stomach while he knelt beside her, holding back her hair.

She grasped onto the seat, resting her head on her arm. He left her propped there long enough to slip into his boxers and wet a washcloth before he picked her up into his arms again.

Like a small child, she let him wash her face, slip off her dress, and slip into his t-shirt. She drank down the aspirin and water he handed her and was asleep before he'd pulled the covers over her.

Jordan grabbed one of the pillows and the blanket from the end of the bed and headed for the couch. This was definitely not the way he'd envisioned her coming to him. It was going to be a long night as he tried to forget how she looked in her red lace bra and barely there panties.

Chapter 14

The following morning, she woke to someone pounding on her head. The pain was intense, and she put her hands over her temples, hoping to make them stop before realizing there was no one there. She cracked open an eye; the sunlight drifting in through the cracks of the blinds sliced her eyes like a knife.

"Chloe!" she shouted, sitting up quickly and immediately regretting it. It took a moment for her to comprehend where she was. What was she doing at Jordan's house? Bits and pieces of last night began to play in her foggy mind, and she groaned aloud.

Dear lord, please tell me I didn't do what I think I did. She looked over at the clock and found a note resting against it.

Chloe is with Mom, so don't worry, she said to rest. There is fresh coffee in the kitchen and two more aspirin beside the bed. I'm on shift, so stay as long as you need. Feel better, J-

Setting the note back down, she slid back under the covers. Pulling the blankets over her head, she groaned, willing this to be a bad dream. If it wasn't, she'd shown up at Jordan's place sloppy drunk and threw herself at him. She squeezed her eyes shut and opened them slowly. She lifted the covers off of her head and looked around again.

It was true; she was in Jordan's bed, wearing his t-shirt, and with little recollection of the night before. She remembered Willow being on Jordan's arm. She'd tried to get off the ship, but had been too late. Tequila.

This was bad. She vaguely remembered knocking on Jordan's door, but not how she'd gotten there. She remembered he'd been naked. Had he opened the door naked? No, he'd been in a towel.

She covered her eyes with her hand as she remembered falling over and pulling his towel down with her.

She knew she should get up, pick up Chloe, and be the responsible mother she signed up to be, but instead she buried deeper into the covers and closed her eyes, breathing in Jordan's familiar scent.

She woke at noon, still feeling like she'd been hit by a large truck, but at least the marching band was no longer doing their halftime show in her head. She took some time to linger in Jordan's large shower and instead of changing back into last night's dress, she threw on the t-shirt she'd slept in and borrowed a pair of his sweats.

She knocked on Betty's door a few minutes after one to pick up her daughter. Betty poured her a glass of iced tea and invited her to sit outside and catch up while Chloe finished her nap.

The sun beamed down on the quaint yard as they sat underneath a large table umbrella. Roses bloomed along the stone fence and jasmine crawled along the opposite side, emitting a powerful scent. She'd always felt so comfortable here, like a part of the family. It was good to know Chloe would grow up with the Wayne's as well.

"I take it things didn't go as planned last night?" Betty finally asked.

"Not even a little bit." Marissa sighed. She didn't want to ask how Betty knew she had "plans" in the first place.

"Do you want to talk about it?"

"I would if I could remember it." She tucked her chin in embarrassment. "I blame Lexie."

Betty rumbled with laughter. "An alcohol-packed night normally means a man's involved."

"It wasn't my best moment." She felt the heat flush her cheeks. "I made a complete fool out of myself."

"Was it Jordan?"

Marissa nodded her head. "He brought a date."

"The two of you have the worst timing." Betty groaned. "It makes me crazy."

"It didn't help my behavior any that his date was Willow Southland."

Betty tapped her chin, seeming to recollect the name. Her eyes suddenly grew large. "Isn't that the girl who made your life miserable in high school?"

"That's the one," she replied. "She still looks amazing, and she's always wanted Jordan. It seems she's finally gotten him."

"Why would Jordan even consider spending time with a girl like her? He's better than that."

"Because she's beautiful, successful, and not an emotional basket case would be my guess. That, and he can't see her black heart through her black lace and perfectly sculpted breasts."

"You're going through a lot. Jordan will see her for what she is soon enough. He's a smart boy. You, on the other hand, although extremely smart, are slow to recognize what's best for you."

Marissa laughed. "Why is it we seem to be our own worst enemies at times? I fell for the wrong man, and wasted so many years of my life."

"You can't think of those years as a waste," Betty scolded.

"I know I shouldn't, but it feels like that sometimes."

"You have to just keep focused on what you want right now. You have to live in the present and let the past go." Betty sipped from her tea. "Do you know what you want now?"

She thought about the question before answering. "Actually, I do. I want to raise my daughter and have a couple more, I want to continue in my career, and…" She paused. "And I want to explore the feelings I'm developing again, or realizing again, for Jordan."

Betty smiled. "Nothing would make me happier than to see you two together."

Marissa just hoped she hadn't blown her chance—again.

Chapter 15

Jordan flipped through the channels, unable to settle on any certain one. Restless, he stood from the couch and turned off the television. He desperately wanted to race to Marissa's house and pull her into his arms. His body was still on fire from the night before, her body covered in only red lace burned into his mind.

Had she really wanted him, or was it the tequila talking? The note she'd left him had been polite, well-mannered Marissa simply thanking him for letting her sleep at his place, for the borrowed t-shirt, and a heartfelt apology for her intoxication. Nothing about wanting to see him, and nothing about what she'd said or offered. Maybe she didn't remember. If she didn't, that would answer his question about whether she meant it or not.

Grabbing his jacket, he headed for the door. He needed to see her, to ask her the questions that plagued him, that wouldn't let him sleep. Opening the door, he ran chest first into Marissa.

"Umm, hi," she mumbled. "I'm sorry, I was just about to knock. I brought your clothes back. And I wanted to thank you again personally for your patience with me last night."

Unsure of what to do with his hands, he tucked them into his pockets. "It was no problem, really. Do you want to come in?"

Her cheeks flushed red and she lowered her head, breaking eye contact. "You were obviously just leaving. I didn't mean to intrude; I should've called first."

Jordan studied her for a moment and was surprised she appeared nervous. "Since when do we call each other before stopping by? Don't be ridiculous, come in."

Without looking up, she walked into the living room and sat down on the couch, still clutching the folded clothes she was returning.

Setting his coat down, he sat down on the couch beside her and waited. He didn't think he'd ever seen her this nervous. She was staring at her lap, picking at a loose thread on his washed and folded shirt. Was she embarrassed she'd shown up drunk, or that she'd shown up at all?

"I'm sorry for last night," she managed to say. "I wasn't quite myself."

He drew his brows together. "Sorry for what part?"

"All of it." Marissa met his gaze.

He had his answer. She hadn't wanted him, it was the tequila that had brought her to his door. He hadn't thought she could still hurt him, but he was wrong. This hurt like hell. But still, he knew he needed to explain himself.

Jordan cleared his throat, and searched for the words he wanted to say. "I wanted to talk to you about the reunion," he managed. "I'm not dating Willow. Well, not really."

Why did he feel like he'd been caught cheating on her? It was making him uncomfortable and he knew he sounded like an idiot.

Marissa looked down. "It's none of my business. You and I are friends."

Frustrated, he reached over and lifted her chin, forcing her to look at him. "Is that all we are, Marissa? After everything, you still refer to us as friends?"

She tried to tilt her head down but he held securely to her chin, keeping her eyes locked with his. He could see her discomfort reflected in her eyes, but he needed to know.

"Is it?" he asked again.

"Yes…no…" She pulled her head free and stared into her lap. "I don't know what to say. You're one of my best friends."

He fought back his urge to yell in frustration. "I'm not arguing that we're friends, Marissa. I'm asking you if that's all we are."

"Steven just died. I don't know, I haven't thought about it." He knew she was lying—she'd never been good at it—but it still hurt.

"Steven's been gone for a long time, even before the car accident, and you know it. This isn't about Steven, and with what he did to you, I don't buy the grieving widow routine," he snapped, his frustration rising to the surface. "If what you say is the truth, then what was last night? Was it strictly the tequila talking? Or were you planning on using me for some sort of retribution?"

Even with her head down, he could see the color rise on her cheeks. Her jaw clenched, and her fingers stopped fidgeting with the loose string. Her head snapped up, and her eyes blazed with anger. "I was married to him for eight years. He lied to me, betrayed me, and humiliated me. He married another woman and had a child with her. But you want to sit here and accuse me of using you for revenge? Revenge on who? Steven?" She rose from the couch and began to pace. "I was drunk and I wasn't thinking. I embarrassed myself because I was jealous you were with Will—" She slapped her hand over her mouth, her eyes wide with surprise.

Jordan felt his heart warm. He wasn't wrong; she did feel something besides friendship for him. He rose to stand in front of her, placing his hands gently on her shoulders.

"I'm sorry Steven hurt you. I'm sorry you feel humiliated, because you shouldn't. But I'm not sorry he's out of your life." He bent his head down trying to see into her eyes. He wasn't surprised to see them filled with tears when she looked up at him. "Marissa, I'll always be your friend. That will never change. But the truth is, I want more."

"Is that why you kissed me?" Her cheeks grew red. "I can't stop thinking about it. Part of me wants to ask you why, and the other part wants to ask you why you haven't done it again."

What could he say? He knew why he'd kissed her, but he wasn't sure he understood why he hadn't done it again.

Her hands straightened the already folded clothes in her arms. "I'm sorry-I shouldn't have said anything." She laughed nervously. "I just can't seem to stop making a fool of myself with you."

Her suddenly shy behavior reminded him again of the girl he'd loved in high school. Removing the clothes from her arms, he set them on the couch and, reaching for her, pulled her against him, buried his hands in her hair, and crushed her mouth with his.

Her body relaxed against him, and a groan of pleasure escaped from her throat, sending his pulse racing. His tongue lightly danced with hers, as the need for her increased. Continuing to kiss her, he gently lowered her on the couch, his body hovering above hers as he ran his hands down her sides and over the swell of her breasts.

His cell phone rang, shattering the silence, and he reached over to silence it. He kissed her again, gently running his tongue over her bottom lip, before deepening the kiss. Lying over her on the couch, he felt like a teenage boy again, making out with the girl from his fantasies.

He opened his eyes to gaze at her, her long, dark lashes fanned out across her cheek, and her lips were red and swollen from his kisses. Her eyes fluttered open when his phone rang for the second time.

Frustrated, he reached up and answered. "Scott, this better be life and death," he shouted to his fellow officer. He got up and held out his finger, signaling he'd only be a minute, and walked into his bedroom, closing the door behind him.

Scott had attended the police academy with him and they'd remained friends even after Scott had taken a job in Los Angeles while he chose to stay in Carmel. Scott was now Internal Affairs and the case he was investigating had branched out too close to home for Jordan's comfort. He hated that he had to keep secrets he didn't want to keep.

"Have you found anything yet?" Scott asked.

"I haven't, not yet," he whispered. "I can't talk now."

"This is bigger than I thought, Wayne. Much bigger. I need you on this one. I need to connect the dots." Scott sounded exasperated.

"I told you I was working on it," Jordan said through clenched teeth. He ran his hand through his hair and paced the floor at the foot of the bed.

"I agreed to avoid the warrant and let you handle it on your end as a personal favor—"

"I know. I said I'd handle it and I will."

He hung up the phone and sat on the bed, resting his head in his hands. Marissa would never forgive him if she knew.

Resigned, he walked back into the living room.

"Everything okay?" she asked.

He forced a reassuring smile. "Just work. Everything is fine."

With the flush still on her cheeks, he wanted to pull her to him and pick up where they'd left off, but the reality of how fragile things were between them held him back. He wanted to do things right this time.

"Have dinner with me Friday night?"

She smiled. "I can do that."

"And wear the red lingerie," he added with a wink.

Chapter 16

Marissa yawned and poured herself a cup of coffee, taking it with her to get into the shower before Chloe woke up. She couldn't help but see the irony in the fact she was raising Steven's child like she'd always imagined. Only she wouldn't have ever believed it would be his child with another wife.

She had just turned off the water when the shower curtain suddenly opened. Startled, she jumped, barely managing to maintain her footing. Chloe stood beside the tub with a bright smile on her sleepy face.

"Good morning, sweet girl." She wrapped herself in a towel and stepped out of the shower to pick up her daughter. Chloe snuggled into her neck and sighed with contentment. At that moment Marissa knew, as much as none of it made any logical sense, this was meant to be. She was meant to be Chloe's mother, regardless of how they came to be together.

A few hours later, after dropping off Chloe and finishing her morning rounds, she tiptoed into Annie's room. As if sensing her presence, Annie slowly opened her eyes.

"What took you so long?" she asked, smiling weakly. "I've been waiting for you. I want to hear all about your date with the handsome fella who has you all aflutter."

"It wasn't a date," Marissa clarified, picking up a brush and gently running it through Annie's hair. "It was our high school reunion, and his sister was my date."

Ignoring her, Annie continued, "Did he look dapper in his suit?"

"He did." Marissa smiled.

"Did he gasp when he got a look at you in your fancy dress?"

Marissa wasn't sure why, but she suddenly felt it was important to let Annie have her moment of fantasy. The truth wasn't romantic or wistful but she believed it could've been had she not chosen to be dishonest with herself where Jordan was concerned. "He did. We danced all night, and as we were coming into port, we walked outside onto the deck." She was starting to enjoy her make-believe story. "He wrapped his suit coat around my shoulders and pulled me against his chest. We just stood there in silence, watching the lights come into view."

Annie's eyes drooped. "And then?" she said quietly.

Marissa closed her eyes and imagined what would have happened next in an ideal scenario. "He placed his hands on my shoulders and turned me around to face him. And then he kissed me until my knees grew weak."

With her eyes still closed, Annie whispered, "My Charlie made my knees weak and my heart pound until the day he died. It's nice, isn't it?"

"It really is." Marissa set the brush down and quietly slipped out of the room. Annie had fallen asleep.

Marissa worked her last few hours, updating her charts and leaving instructions for the next shift on the white board. She'd just entered the lobby area when Betty came in the front door with Chloe, who was crying uncontrollably and fighting to get out of her arms. Betty looked frazzled and Marissa rushed over to take Chloe.

"I don't know what happened," Betty said. "She was sleeping in the car, and the minute we pulled up in the parking lot she started to scream and fought me to put her down. I've never seen her like this."

Marissa hadn't either. Chloe squirmed and grunted, bending backward in an attempt to get out of her grasp. Afraid she would drop her, Marissa set her down and took her hands, trying to calm her.

"What's wrong, sweetheart?" she said in a soothing tone. "Tell Mommy what's wrong."

Chloe pulled her hands away and ran down the hall as quickly as her baby legs would let her. Marissa shot up and hurried after her. Chloe's crying grew louder, almost heart wrenching the farther she got down the hall. Chloe stopped outside of Annie's room and held her hand against the wood door. She hung her head, her howling changing to a whimper as she struggled to push open the heavy door.

Marissa opened the door for her and let her rush inside. She didn't think she could stop her even if she tried. She followed her into the dimly lit room.

Chloe walked over to the bed, tears streaming down her reddened cheeks and took Annie's hand.

"Annie..."

Marissa's mouth dropped open in amazement. It was the first time she'd heard Chloe speak. On the heels of that revelation, she noticed how still the room was, and her chest tightened and her eyes welled up with tears. Annie was gone.

She picked up her daughter and sat on the edge of the bed with her on her lap. Chloe reached over and gently touched Annie's still face and turning, burrowed into Marissa's chest and began to sob again.

Marissa sat beside her friend, consoling her daughter, and wondering how Chloe could have possibly known.

Chapter 17

Jordan took a deep breath before knocking on Marissa's front door. He wanted to check on Chloe, see for himself she was alright, and he needed to see Marissa. She'd always taken it hard when she lost a patient, but Annie was special and had meant so much to her.

The door opened and before he could speak, Marissa threw herself into his arms and held him tight. "I feel so selfish," she cried. "I know she's in a better place and finally free from her pain, but I want her here. I'm going to miss her so much."

"You're not selfish," he soothed. "You loved her. I think it's understandable you would want her to stay."

She stepped back, and a small, grateful smile crossed her face. "I'm glad you're here." She let him enter, and in the light of the foyer he could see her eyes were red and swollen from crying. Strands of her hair had fallen from its clip, and she was still in her scrubs from work.

Closing the door behind him, he slipped off his coat and hung it on the rack beside hers. "How is Chloe?"

Marissa headed for the living room and switched on a lamp beside the couch. "She's finally sleeping," she said, pulling her legs under herself in the corner of the couch. She turned to him once he'd sat down beside her. "It was so strange. It was like Chloe knew. She was sobbing and fighting to get down. I'd never seen her that way. She ran down the hall and struggled to get into Annie's room."

"That's what Mom said," he added. "Chloe knew the minute they pulled into the parking lot something was wrong."

"She spoke, Jordan." Marissa's amber eyes lost some of their grief. "She said Annie's name. It was the most beautiful, and at the same time heart-wrenching, sound."

"It's strange the way the two of them connected. From what you've told me, it was like they'd always known each other."

"It was," she agreed. "Annie told me Chloe was special. I still wonder what she actually meant."

"You and I know she's special," Jordan said gently, "but it sounds like Annie meant it in a deeper way. Like she saw something nobody else could."

Marissa sighed and nodded her head. "Their connection was incredible."

"Are you holding up okay? You've been through so much recently." He took hold of her hand.

She leaned over and rested her head against his shoulder. "I will be fine. You think I'd be used to this by now."

"You'll never be used to it; your heart is too big. Besides, Annie was your friend."

She wiped her eyes and sniffed. "She was amazing."

"In light of everything, we can just reschedule Friday."

She lifted her head and looked at him. "Would I be a terrible person if I said I didn't want to reschedule? That I still want to have our date?"

He kissed her lightly on the lips. "Not at all. And selfishly I'm glad. I didn't want to wait any longer to be alone with you."

Walking into the foyer, he slipped on his coat before turning back to her. "And I'm very sorry about your loss. I know what Annie meant to you."

They both turned around when another voice filled the room.

"Mama," Chloe said, standing on the other side of the baby gate at the top of the stairs.

Marissa turned to look at him, her eyes filled with tears and the biggest smile he'd ever seen on her face. He kissed her on the cheek and let himself out, grateful he'd been there to witness that moment.

Chapter 18

Marissa woke Friday morning with the comforting feeling of her daughter snuggled next to her. Her daughter—she liked the sound of that. Even in light of losing Annie, she felt such happiness with the changes in her life the last few months.

And to top it off, she had a date with Jordan tonight. It was a date, wasn't it? Of course it was, he told her to wear lingerie. She giggled to herself and placed her hand over her mouth to stifle it when Chloe stirred beside her.

After scrambled eggs—Chloe's favorite—and a race to get out of the house, Marissa walked through the front door of the Talbot House with only two minutes to spare. She was surprised to see Emily Sinclair in the hallway.

"Emily," Marissa greeted her. "I wasn't expecting you today. What a nice surprise." Embracing her boss and friend, she smiled. This was the exact boost she needed.

"I'm so sorry to hear about Annie," Emily said. "I know how much you loved her."

"I know she's in a better place, and no longer in pain," she said, then sighed. "But I'm going to miss her so much. I don't know how I'm going to convince myself to enter her room."

"I think it will be hard for all of us." Emily wiped a tear from her eye.

"What brings you in from the city?"

"Actually, I've come to talk to you. Do you have a moment we can speak in private?" her friend asked.

Marissa held open the door to the small break room and waited for Emily to enter. "Is everything okay?"

"I'm taking care of Annie's last wishes and her burial requests. You know she didn't have any family."

Marissa nodded her head.

"She left her trust to the foundation, and has requested when the time comes, the foundation pays for Chloe's college."

She gasped. "Why would she do that?"

"She didn't say, but she left a sealed, confidential envelope for you."

Marissa's mind was spinning. She'd told her about leaving her trust to the foundation. She'd been so proud she could give back to the place she felt "was like family."

Emily handed over the envelope addressed to her in Annie's familiar scrawl. She felt the sting behind her eyes as the tears pooled.

"I'll leave you to read her letter. Please find me before you start your rounds."

Marissa continued to stare down at the envelope she clutched. After Emily had closed the door tightly behind her, she picked it up and gently opened the sealed flap.

My dear Marissa,

If you're reading this, I've finally joined my Charlie in heaven. Don't cry for me, I've waited a long time for this moment. Know that I'm happy. You have been a bright light in my life and I'm grateful to have been blessed by your friendship. The Lord may not have blessed me with a daughter of my own, but I'm thankful he saw my need for you, and more, recognized your need for Chloe.

I expect no argument regarding my decision to pay for Chloe's college. Of this I insist. Know that I'm of sound mind, and I want her to live her dreams. I don't know how or what, or even why, but I know our Chloe is going to touch many lives.

She's a special girl, Marissa, and put on this earth to be with you. All lives are destined, and her arrival in your life was fate. You must stay strong and never give up. Be happy. My love, Annie

Marissa wiped the tears from her cheeks and read the letter again before locating Emily and sharing the contents of the letter with her.

"She didn't give any reason for her decision."

Emily chuckled. "Annie always got what she wanted."

Marissa smiled wistfully and nodded her head.

"I almost forgot," Emily handed her another envelope. "It's an invitation to Bob and my engagement party. We both hope you can make it."

"I wouldn't miss it," Marissa tucked the invitation into her pocket. "I still can't believe you're getting married."

"I can't either," Emily beamed. "I can't believe how happy I am. I can't remember the last time I felt this way."

Marissa felt a small tug in her chest. *Someday*, she thought, *someday I will be that happy. I hope.*

Chapter 19

Standing outside Jordan's door, Marissa almost wished she had the same liquid courage as the night of the reunion. Her palms were sweaty, and her stomach was holding its own gymnastics competition. No matter how many times she reminded herself it was only Jordan, she still wasn't convinced. This wasn't just a friendly stop over like in the past—this was different. Hell, this time she was in red lace panties.

Jordan opened the door with the same friendly smile he always did, but this time she noticed his eyes drift from her head to her toes. She suddenly didn't know what to do with her hands. Nervously, she ran them down the front of the simple, black dress she'd decided on after tearing through her closet like a woman possessed. Yes, this was definitely different.

"Come on in." Jordan stood back. "You look beautiful."

Finding her tongue frozen, she simply smiled and walked past him, setting her purse on the island counter. The routine was so familiar, why were her knees buckling?

Jordan sauntered around the counter and lifted the lid to the pot on the stove. The scent of garlic and fresh tomatoes wafted through the kitchen, and he waved the steam toward her.

Her eyes grew wide with recognition. "Is that your famous linguini and clam sauce?"

His eyebrows flicked up and down in response. Dipping a large wooden spoon into the sauce, he leaned over the counter and offered her a taste.

She closed her eyes and moaned appreciatively. In slow motion she opened her eyes. She'd never before seen a look like the one on Jordan's face—he seemed frozen with the spoon still at her mouth. His deep green eyes grew darker, sharper, his gaze intense. His mouth was faintly open, his breathing slightly labored. Locking her eyes with his, she felt her body lean toward him as if pulled by an invisible rope.

He dropped the spoon and it clanked against the counter, shattering the silence. Jordan came around the counter quickly and crushed his mouth to hers. The breath she'd held exploded from her lungs when he reached down and lifted her into his arms.

"This is happening," he mumbled, walking quickly toward his bedroom.

Marissa felt a moment of panic and lifted a hand to his chest. As if sensing her hesitation, he bent his lips to hers and hurried his steps. His kisses made her dizzy, and her body caught fire.

He laid her gently across the bed, his lips still closed over hers. His tongue explored, stroked, and then gently drew back, softly tasting her swollen lips. His body hovered above hers, his hands burrowed into her hair as he kissed and suckled a trail down her neck and across her collarbone.

Her body arched against his, and she ran her hands down his spine. He moaned when she slid her fingers beneath his shirt and applied more pressure as she worked her way up his back.

Skimming his hands down her sides, he slowly drew up the bottom of her dress. She felt his body stiffen when his hands reached the top of her stockings and met the warmth of her thigh. "Marissa," he purred.

Rising, he stood at the side of the bed and gazed at her. The light from the living room filtered through the open door, and she could see the desire in his eyes. She sat up and watched as he tugged his shirt over his head, his hard chest lightly covered in perspiration. Scrambling to her knees, she reached out and ran her fingers through the patch of soft, dark hair that covered his chest and stroked her palms over his nipples.

His body had changed since they'd been high schoolers and her hands itched to discover him once again. She reached around to pull down the zipper on her dress and was surprised when Jordan reached out and stopped her.

"I want to undress you," he told her in a deep, husky voice.

His arms came around her and he lowered the zipper on her black dress. Taking a step back, he slid the straps from her shoulders and sucked in his breath when it fell around her knees, leaving her in only stockings and red lace.

She had a moment of self-consciousness and her arms instinctively crossed over herself.

"Don't." His eyes rose to meet hers, and the hunger she saw in their depth empowered her.

Uncrossing her arms, she watched as he lowered his gaze and reached behind her to unclasp her bra. Taking his time, he slid it down her arms and let it drop to the floor. His eyes devoured her, but he didn't touch her. Overcome with need, her body arched toward him. Stepping closer, he pulled her into his arms and took her mouth with his. Marissa reached up and dug her fingers into his thick, dark hair, urging him to kiss her deeper.

The feel of his chest massaging against her breasts and the sensation of the friction against her sensitive nipples snapped the last of her control. Breathless, she reached out to unhook the button on his jeans. Following his example, she slid them down his legs and ran her hands back up to his waist.

Jordan stepped out of his jeans until he stood naked in front of her. In one rapid movement, he yanked back the comforter on the bed and laid her against the cool sheets. Leaning over her, he placed his fingers beneath the thin straps of her lace panties and teased them down her legs.

"You are so beautiful," he said breathlessly.

Lowering himself over her, he took his time running his hands over every inch of her body, leaving a scorching trail. She couldn't remember a time she'd ever felt such a strong need for a man. Her body ached for him, arching to be closer, to feel his skin against hers.

Her hips lifted from the bed, her hands urging him to stop his torment. He looked up at her, a knowing smile on his face, before following the same path down her body his hands had traveled, only this time using his lips and tongue.

He brought her over the edge, her body shuddering with pleasure. Before she could catch her breath, he began the exquisite torture again.

"Jordan, please," she begged, her nails digging into the soft flesh of his back.

He kissed and caressed his way back up her body, his hands trailing up her sides. Lowering his body against hers, he bent down and pressed his lips to hers. He lifted his head and her eyes fluttered open, locking with his. Watching her, he made love to her slowly, driving her wild with need for him. Surprising herself, Marissa wrapped her arms around him, rolled him onto his back and took control until they both crested together.

An hour later, she lay comfortably in his arms, her body still humming. She shifted and rose up on her elbow, stroking his chest with her hand. He smiled but didn't open his eyes.

"I could get *very* used to this."

She ran a finger in a circle around each nipple, watching his face, pleased with the change in his breathing. She knew she could get used to it as well. They'd come a long way since the groping, clueless teens they'd been before.

"Jordan?" she purred.

"Hmmm?"

"Are you ready to go again?"

His eyes opened wide, and a seductive smile crossed his face. "Insatiable. My kind of woman," he said, rolling over and reaching for her.

She put her hand against his chest, stopping him. "Not so fast."

His brows drew together and his lips turned down in a boyish pout.

"You have to feed me first. I'm starving," she stated. "And my mouth is watering because I can still smell our dinner."

Jordan threw his head back and laughed as he climbed from the bed. Pulling herself up against the pillows, she grinned and watched him walk into the kitchen in all of his naked glory.

Chapter 20

Jordan couldn't stop smiling. Or get the vision of Marissa lying beneath him, her skin glowing, her eyes glazed, his name on her lips, out of his mind. Last night was everything he'd ever dreamed it would be and more.

Walking into the reception area at the station, he slammed directly into Grayson.

"Geez, Wayne, didn't mean to get in your way," his brother-in-law said sarcastically. "Where's your head at?"

Snapping back into focus, Jordan dipped his head. "Good morning, Hunter," he replied, heading for his office.

He sat down at his desk and looked up when Grayson filled the doorway, leaning casually against the frame, his legs crossed at the ankle and a knowing smile on his face.

"You were with a woman last night," his partner said smugly. "And by the dazed look on your face, my bet it was finally Marissa."

Jordan felt his mouth drop open before slamming it closed again. "Don't you have work to do?" he asked, picking up a stack of papers on his desk and pretending to read the top page.

Instead of leaving as he'd hoped, Grayson walked into the office and closed the door behind him before settling into the chair across from Jordan's desk. Jordan looked up and scowled at the smug look on his partner's face.

"This isn't the ladies room, Hunter. Don't expect me to giggle and share details with you regarding my personal life."

"I knew it!" Grayson slapped his thigh and laughed. "Wait until I tell Lexie. She's going to flip."

Clenching his jaw, Jordan took a deep breath. "What exactly would you be telling Lexie that would make her 'flip'?"

"Are you kidding me?" Grayson sat forward in his chair, his arms resting on his thighs. "For years Lexie's been trying to predict when you two would figure it out." He laughed. "She was convinced after your stunt with Willow, it was going to be a long time before Marissa gave you another shot."

Jordan drew his brows together. "What do you mean, another shot? High school was a long time ago."

He wasn't happy to know his sister was discussing his relationship—or non-relationship as it were—with his partner. He didn't care if Grayson was her husband. His life was nobody's business.

"She was sure the night of your reunion would be the turning point for you two," Grayson said. "You sure loused that up."

Jordan jerked his head. Marissa told Lexie what happened? Damn, women really did tell each other everything.

"I didn't louse it up," he shouted. "What kind of man takes advantage of a woman who is so drunk she can't stand up? Even if he really wanted to."

Grayson appeared shocked. "Marissa came to the reunion drunk? That doesn't sound like her."

"No, my place—"

"Wait," his brother-in-law cut in. "Marissa came to your place drunk and stumbling? When?" His eyes grew large. "The night of the reunion? Lexie said she dropped Marissa off at home. She went to your place afterward?"

Realizing Marissa hadn't told Lexie, Jordan scowled. "Never mind about that part," he barked. "What did you mean I loused it up the night of the reunion?"

"When you showed up with Willow." Grayson furrowed his brow. "Marissa hates Willow, always has from what I hear, and you march in with her on your arm the night Marissa decides to step it up."

Step it up? Had Marissa been hoping to be with him that night? He tried to remember any signs of jealousy or anger from her. Lexie hadn't been subtle—not that she was capable of it—in her disgust with his date choice, but he couldn't recall any signs from Marissa. Instead, all he could picture was how beautiful she had looked, and the red lace she'd worn beneath that dress.

"Your sister cursed your name for days afterward. Well, yours and Willow's, but mainly yours. She is still referring to you as a clueless dumbass, but I think after she hears about last night, you might be forgiven."

Jordan groaned. "Why does Lexie have to be Marissa's best friend? My life would be so much easier if my sister weren't an opinionated busybody who also believes nobody in her life is capable of having a relationship without her guidance."

"That's our girl," Grayson agreed cheerfully. "It's got to irritate the hell out of you that she's usually right."

Resting his head on the palm of his hand, Jordan sighed. "If you had any sense of decency, you'd be keeping my secrets instead of getting excited when there is gossip for you to share with Lexie. You're worse than a woman. You feed her the ammunition she needs to stay permanently lodged in the middle of my business."

"Maybe, but it keeps me out of trouble. You of all people know how widespread the effect is when Lexie is bored and without someone else's life to meddle in. This is self-preservation—you happen to be my sacrifice this week."

Jordan couldn't help but laugh. "I've always questioned your sanity. That girl's a handful. But I must admit, I admire your ability to skillfully get around her."

"I like her feistiness." Then winking, he added, "It makes for great—"

"Stop right there, Hunter," he interrupted.

His partner rose from the chair and left the office still laughing.

Chapter 21

The morning of Annie's funeral was bright and sunny, but the mood in the kitchen was anything but. Chloe sat in her high chair pushing eggs around her plate but not putting any in her mouth. When Marissa spoke to her, she would look up, no emotion on her face. Her mother's heart broke to see how much losing Annie had affected her daughter.

Just as she'd feared, Chloe cried, screamed, and kicked when Marissa attempted to drop her off at Betty's so she could attend the funeral. Wasn't two years old too young for a funeral? But with Chloe's attachment to Annie, would it be wrong to leave her behind? The right decision eluded her.

As if reading her mind, Betty reached over and put her hand supportively on Marissa's shoulder. "You should take her."

"I think you're right."

"You can always call me to pick her up if it becomes too much for her." Betty stroked Chloe's head, smoothing down her soft, blonde curls.

Leaning in, Marissa placed a kiss on Betty's cheek. "I don't know what I'd do without you."

The woman's cheeks turned pink. "You would be fine. You're the strongest woman I know."

Fifteen minutes later, they arrived at the tiny white church overlooking a valley filled with brightly colored wild-flowers. Marissa knew this was the same church Annie had married Charlie in, as well as the church where she held his funeral, and where she wanted be laid to rest beside him.

The church was mainly empty, as Annie had outlived most of the people in her life, but the staff, who'd become Annie's friends, were there to say their goodbyes.

Emily stood by the open doors, welcoming each visitor personally. Her face lit up when Marissa and Chloe reached the top of the church steps.

"Everything looks beautiful. You've done Annie proud."

Emily blushed and turned to scan the church. Colorful wildflowers filled glass vases, making it appear as though the valley had spread inside. There was a picture board on each side of the casket with photos showcasing Annie's life; her smile glowing from each photo.

"Thank you." Emily embraced her. "As much as I'll miss her, it warms my heart to know she is finally free of her pain, and back with the man she loved above all else."

Chloe began to squirm in her arms, and Emily reached for her, cradling her and kissing the top of her head. Chloe kissed her back, causing Emily to giggle with pride. "She remembers me."

"Of course she does," Marissa rubbed her daughter's back.

Twisting around, Chloe used her arms to push against Emily in an attempt to get down.

"I can't tell you how much she resembles the way I pictured Aimee as a child at that age, all those blonde curls and pink cheeks. Not to mention a strong will." Emily set her down, and both women watched as she made her way to the front of the church.

She stopped at the picture board and just stood staring at it. Another small group of people arrived and Marissa excused herself. Chloe reached out her arms when she approached, and she pulled her against her chest. The child nuzzled into her neck, her cheeks wet with tears. Marissa rocked her and tried to soothe her as her own eyes filled with tears at her daughter's heartache.

Still cradling Chloe, she sat next to Lexie in the front pew as the pastor stepped behind the podium and began the service.

By the time they'd finished the testimonials and began to file out behind Annie's casket, there wasn't a dry eye in the church.

Annie had touched a lot of lives in the short time she stayed with them. Not to mention a little girl, who was still shaking and crying in Marissa's arms.

The breeze carried the sweet smell of flowers as the small group gathered around Annie's casket to lay her to rest beside her husband. A beautiful black woman in a choir gown sang *Amazing Grace* as each of them stood to place a single rose on top of her casket.

Chloe jumped from Marissa's lap and held out her hand. A lump formed in her throat as she handed her the single rose. The small group watched as Chloe stopped beside Annie's casket with one hand touching the wood and tears streaming down her face.

Marissa stepped forward and lifted Chloe, and her tiny hand gently laid the rose down beside the others.

Chapter 22

After two weeks, Chloe had finally stopped crying herself to sleep at night. Marissa was grateful Chloe seemed to be coming back from that dark place she'd been since Annie died.

She was excited about their drive to the city tonight for Emily Sinclair and Bob's engagement party. She pulled into the driveway at Jordan's parents' house, who were keeping both Chloe and their grandson, Ryan, for the night. Judging by the number of cars in the driveway, she was the last to arrive.

Before she could lift Chloe from the car seat, Jordan walked up behind her and held his arms out. Chloe smiled and reached for him, wrapping her tiny arms around his neck and kissing him on the cheek.

"Hey, beautiful." He kissed her cheek, the top of her head, and continued to her forehead, and all along her face causing her to laugh uncontrollably.

Marissa flung Chloe's bag onto her shoulder and closed and locked the car door. Turning around she smiled at Jordan standing in front of her with his lips puckered for a kiss. Leaning in, she kissed him gently.

He whispered into her ear, "You're lucky there's a child present. You smell amazing and I'm picturing you on the hood of your car right now."

She could feel the heat on her cheeks and bent her head down pretending to search for something in her purse. It was obvious Jordan didn't buy it when he headed for the house, and his laughter drifted behind him.

Almost two hours later they pulled in through the gates of the Sinclair Estate. Grayson tossed his keys to the parking attendant and opened the door for Lexie, while Jordan held out his hand to help Marissa from the backseat. Before they were up the porch stairs the large ornate door opened and Emily's daughter, Aimee, and her husband, Mark, rushed through it.

"You're finally here," Aimee squealed, throwing her arms around each of them for a hug. "I've missed you so much."

Aimee had become a dear friend since they worked together on a major fundraiser for the Talbot Foundation. The three of them—Lexie, Aimee, and herself—tried to get together at least once a month to catch up, but with everything happening in her life, it hadn't been possible and it seemed like forever since Marissa had seen her.

They stepped aside as a man in a dark suit walked up carrying their overnight bags. He nodded his head at them and continued through the door and up the stairs to place their bags into their rooms.

Mark turned back to Jordan and Grayson. "Let's go find a cold beer and let these girls catch up."

Aimee reached over and grasped Mark's arm. "I can't wait any longer, can we do it now?"

A smile lit Mark's face as he nodded at his wife.

"We have something to show all of you," Aimee told them, unable to conceal her excitement.

The small group headed up the stairs behind Mark and Aimee and followed them to their personal wing of the estate. Stopping in front of one of the doors, Aimee turned around, her face beaming and holding tightly to Mark's hand.

"Ready?"

"Yes! You're killing me here," Lexie stepped forward impatiently.

Mark opened the door and they all filed into a nursery with soft yellow walls, painted with vines and ladybugs along the middle. There was a dark wood crib with fluffy white bedding and a mobile reaching over the side with small stuffed ladybugs hanging from white ribbon.

Turning to Aimee, Marissa asked, "Does this mean what I think it means?" She smiled at the proud look on Mark's face.

Aimee bounced up and down. "We're pregnant. Mark and I are finally going to start our family."

Marissa felt a moment of jealousy. She had Chloe, and she couldn't be happier, but deep down inside, she knew she wanted just a touch of what her friends had. Now with both of her friends expecting she realized again how much time she'd wasted in her marriage to Steven.

She looked up when Jordan laid an arm across her shoulders. His eyes were soft, and seemed to know what she was thinking. She tipped her head to his shoulder, enjoying the comfort of his embrace.

"Mom is so excited." Aimee gushed. "You can tell she was the one who decorated the nursery."

"Emily has a knack for decorating," Lexie said. "I may have to beg her to come and do mine."

When they reached the bottom of the stairs, Mimsey, the Sinclair's cook and adopted family member, came around the corner and scowled at them.

"Turn right around and go get dressed," she ordered. "Miss Emily's party starts in less than an hour and I expect the lot of you to be dressed and ready to welcome her guests."

The six of them turned and headed back upstairs, giggling and sassing under their breath like a group of teenagers.

● ● ●

An hour later, they were dressed and ready as instructed.

Jordan walked over to the small waterfall flowing into a koi pond. There was a bridge over the pond with palm trees surrounding the far side. Lights were strung across the bridge and small lily pads holding lit candles floated on the water.

He smiled when Marissa approached to stand beside him. Turning to her, he tilted her chin and kissed her.

"You look beautiful."

That was an understatement. She took his breath away. She wore a silk dress in a soft mint shade that fell longer in the back, allowing the front to show off her beautiful, long legs. It fell from thin straps and scooped low enough to give him a small glimpse of the curve of her breasts. She wore a small silver chain around her wrist and silver sandals on her feet. Her auburn hair had been clipped back, with soft tendrils falling around her face and blowing gently in the wind.

She took his hand. "Want to buy me a drink, good looking?"

Winking at her, he twined his fingers with hers and led her toward the tented bar area. Drinks in hand they sat down at one of the rod iron tables scattered across the yard, and within seconds they were joined by their friends.

They were still discussing pregnancy and children. Jordan paid only half attention to what they were saying as his mind drifted and he imagined walking along the beach with Chloe on his shoulders, holding tightly to Marissa's hand as she waddled beside him, pregnant with their child.

Startled, he jumped when Mark grabbed his shoulder. "You didn't hear a word I said, did you?"

"I never listen to a word you say. Why would now be any different?" Jordan shrugged his shoulders.

Always a good sport, Mark laughed and repeated his question. "How did you finally convince Marissa to give you the time of day?"

"I'm only using him for his body," Marissa teased.

"Nice, very nice," Jordan shook his head. "Now it makes sense." He tried to appear hurt, but as the others began to laugh, he couldn't keep up the charade. He turned to Marissa and said, "And just to let you know, I'm perfectly okay with that."

"Marissa, how are you? I've been thinking about all of the changes in your life lately." Aimee's green eyes filled with genuine sympathy.

Jordan couldn't help but eavesdrop even as he pretended to be engaged in the conversation the men were having next to him.

"It has been a very interesting couple of months," Marissa tried to laugh, but her voice choked. "It hasn't been easy, but I'm making it through."

"Have you considered possibly seeing a counselor to help you work through this?" Aimee asked.

"Oh she worked through it alright." Lexie wiggled her eyebrows.

Jordan groaned inwardly.

"What does that mean?" Aimee asked.

"Our calm, cool, and composed girl dumped all of Steven's belongings in her front yard. She smashed pictures, his computer, and all of his trophies," Lexie said proudly.

"You did?" This time it was Aimee's mouth dropping open in surprise.

Marissa blushed.

Aimee just laughed. "I can picture it. Any woman would've thought about doing that in your position."

"I would've probably burned the house down," Lexie volunteered.

"In all honesty, I'm a little disappointed you got to trash his things and I didn't get to help." Aimee frowned.

"She didn't call me either and I still haven't forgiven her."

"What is so funny over here?"

All of them turned to Emily.

"Oh my God, you look so beautiful." Aimee's eyes filled with tears and she rose to hug her mother.

"Wow!" Lexie added.

"Oh Emily, you look absolutely stunning." Marissa wiped her eyes.

Jordan watched as Emily turned in a slow circle to show her back. It was bare, with a scoop of white silk resting just above her hips. She was a beautiful woman, no man could argue that.

"Too much?" she asked, picking a glass of champagne from the tray of a waiter.

"Am I the luckiest man alive, or what?" Bob, Emily's fiancé, came up beside her. "You are ravishing," he said, bending to kiss her. "And this gorgeous vision is going to be my wife in three short months." Bob wrapped his arm around her.

Jordan watched as the band began to play and Bob escorted Emily onto the floor. Next to his parents, he couldn't remember a happier couple. You could feel the love they had for each other.

He wondered if Marissa was feeling any of the symbolism he was. Emily had lost her husband at a young age and never believed she'd ever find love again. But after close to twenty-five years, she'd been reunited with her daughter and found love with Bob. Would Marissa ever be able to let go of her hurts and trust in them? He hoped so.

Refusing to dwell on something he couldn't correct right now, he stepped up beside her and handed her a glass of champagne. "It's nice to see them together." He smiled as Bob effortlessly spun Emily around the floor. "They've waited so long for each other. They deserve a long life of happiness."

She smiled and nodded her head. As the waiter removed their empty glasses, Jordan held out his arm to her. "May I have the pleasure of this dance?"

"You may," she responded, dipping her head to him.

With a smile on his face, the stars shining brightly overhead, and the intoxicating scent of the rose garden on the warm breeze, Jordan held Marissa in his arms and danced the night away.

Chapter 23

The party had been beautiful. Marissa sat on the edge of the king-size bed in one of the many guest rooms and pulled off her heels. Her room had been readied, her suitcase unpacked, and the covers pulled down on the bed. The light beside the bed was on low and candles were lit all around the room creating a soft glow. Sated, slightly tipsy, and more relaxed then she'd been in months, she sighed in contentment and flopped back across the bed.

"You're so beautiful."

She jumped and sucked in a breath, her hand automatically slapping against her chest to stop her heart from beating through. "You scared me."

Jordan sat down beside her on the bed. He ran his hands through her hair, releasing the clips that held it up. "I've been waiting to do this all evening."

She watched his face as he continued to stroke his hands through her long hair. Intent on his journey, he brushed his thumb along her face and across her lips. The look in his eyes as he studied her caused her pulse to race, and flames of desire to shoot through her. She closed her eyes and let her head fall softly against his hand.

His hands came to rest on both sides of her face, his lips playing with hers. Burying her hands into his hair she pulled him closer, wanting to feel him against her, to kiss him deeper.

"Not yet," he whispered against her lips.

Jordan suckled on her bottom lip, and ran his tongue softly over them, slipping inside to play with hers. A moan of desire escaped her lips. She felt him stiffen and knew he fought for control.

Kissing a path along her neck, he slid the strap from her shoulder and followed it with his tongue, moving across her chest to the swell of her breast. Her head rolled back, and she pushed her chest out wanting more.

He lifted her to her knees, sliding her dress over her head. Without taking his eyes from her, he unbuttoned his shirt and tossed it to the floor beside her dress. She remained on her knees wearing only her white lace panties and watched him undress. She put her hand out to touch him, but he pulled back, denying her.

"Not yet," he said again, his voice hoarse with desire.

Fire surged through her body, and her control was slipping as he crawled onto the bed, his naked body glistening in the candlelight. He stopped in front of her and ran his hands the length of her body, leaving a heated trail everywhere he touched.

Laying her gently onto the bed, he continued to touch her, following his hands with his mouth and tongue. He suckled her breast, running his tongue in a slow circle around her nipple. She began to writhe beneath his touch, aching for more.

He moved down her body, kissing her inch by inch. Unable to fight it, she dug her hands into his hair and called out his name, her begging voice filled with need. He rolled above her and kissed her again. She moved with him as they both reached their finish together.

Unable to move her weakened body, she purred as he pulled her into his arms and drew the covers over her. She was asleep before he'd turned out the light.

Chapter 24

Marissa opened the door, surprised to see Chloe's caseworker, Diane Williams, on her doorstep—and more so to see Jordan standing beside her. "I wasn't expecting you until next week. Please don't tell me I wrote it down wrong." She invited them inside.

"Jordan, what brings you out this afternoon? Two surprises on my doorstep at once." Marissa closed the door behind them and led them into the kitchen. "How big of a ding are dishes in the sink?" she chuckled.

Offering them something to drink, she poured each of them a glass of lemonade. "What's going on? Did you two happen to show up on my porch at the same time by coincidence?"

Jordan cleared his throat. "No, I offered to come with Ms. Williams."

The caseworker frowned.

"What's wrong? You're scaring me," she half joked.

"I'm so sorry, Marissa." She looked down, running her finger slowly around the rim of her glass. "I shouldn't have just shown up, but I didn't know if I could get the words out on the phone or I would've warned you. I wanted you to hear it from me."

"Hear what? Warn me?" Marissa trembled, crossing her arms over her chest. She was beginning to think she should never answer her door again. Every time she'd done so lately, it seemed to be bad news, and by the expressions on their faces, this was one of those times.

"They want Chloe," Ms. Williams' voice cracked.

"Who wants Chloe?" she said loudly. Lowering her voice, she asked again, "Who wants Chloe? I don't understand what you mean."

"It's been brought to the attention of the courts that Steven has a half-brother."

"What?" Marissa creased her brow and looked from the caseworker to Jordan. His eyes were sad and filled with pity, and he raked his hand through his hair nervously. "No, he doesn't. I would've known if he had a brother." She filled her lungs with air and slowly blew it out through pursed lips. "Or maybe I wouldn't. It seems there are many things about Steven I wasn't aware of."

Ms. Williams reached over and patted her hand.

"What exactly does this mean? What does it have to do with Chloe?" She could feel her heart pounding faster and the blood drain from her face.

"Because Steven's request wasn't filed with the courts, it isn't legal or binding against a family member. You can fight him in court, and you might even win, but..."

"But, what?"

"But I have to take Chloe back with me. Jack and his wife have already been granted temporary custody."

She leaped from the stool and paced back and forth. "How can they do this? She's finally getting settled in, sleeping through the night, started potty training, and is even beginning to talk. How can they just pull her out of her home?"

"The law isn't always fair." Ms. Williams turned on her stool to track Marissa's movements. "This is the hardest part of my job, knowing the system isn't working in the child's best interest."

"But the law is the law, right?" Marissa felt the heat rising back into her cheeks. She eyed Jordan, clenching her fists, her voice now a snarl. "And is that why you're here? To help them take away my daughter because the law doesn't care if the child is happy and thriving? So what if there are hearts involved and ripped open. Blood is blood, right?"

"Marissa—"

"No, it's wrong! How could I not have known Steven had a brother? They certainly couldn't have been close. Hell, did Steven even know this person existed?" Tears flowed down her cheeks and she struggled to breathe. The pain was almost physical; unbearable. Despair tightened her chest until she felt she might die from it.

Ms. Williams didn't speak but pulled her into her arms. Marissa could feel the caseworker crying with her, and knew she was genuinely upset by the turn of events, but her anger surged.

She pulled back, her hands balled into fists, her teeth clenched together. "I won't let this happen!" she growled. "You can't just show up here and expect me to hand over my daughter to you." Marissa's voice rose and cracked. "This isn't right! And you..." she turned and spat at Jordan, "How dare you! How dare you show up here and...and what...physically rip her out of my arms if I refuse to let this happen? Is that what you're here for, Jordan?"

He jerked back like she'd struck him but remained silent. Tears welled in his eyes as he watched her.

Ms. Williams, with streams of tears rolling down her face, said softly, "I know it's not fair."

The pain was agonizing, like someone had stabbed her in the chest with a dull knife. She bent over, grasping her stomach as the sobs wracked her body. "I can't lose her."

"We will fight this, Marissa. I will fight with you," Jordan mumbled, seeming to find his voice.

She nodded her head, but she didn't believe it. If Steven had a brother, he would be the logical choice to raise Chloe. Even if deep down she knew there was nobody in the world who would love that little girl more than she did.

"When?"

"I can give you a few hours," Ms. Williams said sympathetically.

"Marissa—" Jordan said tenderly.

"Get out, Jordan," she interrupted. She didn't have the strength to yell. "You won't have to arrest me today, so get the hell out of my house."

Hanging her head in defeat, Marissa slowly trudged up the stairs to wake Chloe. In a matter of minutes, she'd lost her daughter with the help of the man she'd believed she was coming to love again.

Her body felt heavy as she stopped outside of the bedroom. She couldn't think about Jordan right now. She wanted every second she could grab before she had to kiss Chloe goodbye for the last time.

Chapter 25

Jordan let himself into his parents' house and set his keys on the table in the foyer. He called out and heard his father respond from the kitchen.

He found his father making a Dagwood sandwich. He hummed as he squirted mustard onto the bread. Without looking up, he offered Jordan half.

"No thanks, Dad," he replied. "I need to get into the boxes you picked up from Marissa's."

His father set his lunch on a plate and turned to meet his eyes. "You okay?"

The stricken look on Marissa's face was etched in his memory. The pain he'd seen in her eyes was unlike anything he'd ever seen before. For a moment he'd worried she would shatter into tiny pieces directly in front of him. It'd been different when he'd told her about Steven. Rage and disbelief would be a welcome reaction versus the defeat and heartbreak she'd been cloaked in.

"No, not really," Jordan confessed. "The state is picking up Chloe from Marissa and taking her to a long-lost brother of Steven's nobody knew about."

Shaking his head, his father let out a low whistle. "That's tough. How's Marissa holding up?"

"Not well. State law requires the caseworker doesn't go alone to these types of situations, and I foolishly thought my presence would make it easier on her. Instead I made it worse and Marissa hates me right now."

"She's hurting; she'll understand what you were trying to do in time. Just be patient."

"I hope you're right," He replied honestly, unable to forget the look of disgust on her face.

"Dad, the boxes?"

"Garage, far left wall." His dad lifted his sandwich and paused. "Why are you looking through her things, son?"

"I'm not looking through her things, I'm looking through his." Jordan cussed under his breath. "I wish I didn't have to do this, but I do. I'd appreciate it if you'd keep this between us for now."

His father simply nodded his head and, picking up his plate, left the kitchen.

Jordan flipped on the light in the garage and looked at the stack of boxes they'd packed up at Marissa's house the night she emptied Steven's den into the front yard. He'd never imagined he would have to go through her personal information. Well, even if it was Steven's information, it still felt horribly wrong.

He wasn't even sure what he was looking for exactly. Maybe he should've let Scott come in with a warrant, but he knew that would only raise more questions. Instead, he volunteered, and now it was more crucial than ever to try and help his colleague connect the dots as he called it. He opened the first box and got started.

Three hours later, he placed the lid on the final box and sighed. He hadn't found much of anything, besides a few canceled checks made out to Steven's half-brother Jack Lowell.

After taking pictures of the front and back of the checks, he put them back in the boxes and let himself out. He needed to call Scott and see what he could do to help. He owed Marissa that.

Chapter 26

For the first time in her life, Marissa understood how someone could die from a broken heart. The pain in her chest was indescribable, she choked on the lump in her throat, and her eyes burned from the tears she couldn't stop.

Chloe had screamed and cried when she'd put her into the car seat in Ms. Williams' car. She could still hear the gut-wrenching sound of her daughter calling out for her in between sobs. How could this be happening? It was more than she could comprehend, and worse, more than she thought she could survive.

She stood in Chloe's room, staring into the now empty closet. In the three months she'd had her, Steven's little girl had become her world. She'd unknowingly filled the void that had always been in her life.

She closed the door to Chloe's room behind her, and grabbing her purse and keys, climbed into her car. She needed to get out of the house. She wanted to drive and drive until the pain stopped, or the nightmare ended.

She wasn't sure how long she'd been on the road, but something inside of her urged her to keep pressing the gas pedal. She finally stopped somewhere in northern California in the middle of nowhere and followed a sign directing her to Shady Pines National Park. She'd rented a cabin for a few days and bought what she needed from the little store attached to the office.

She'd never considered herself one to run from her problems, but as she sat at the end of the dock and let her feet dangle in the water, she knew that was exactly what she'd done.

It was much colder here and she pulled her souvenir sweatshirt closer to her body. The sun set over the lake, and pink and orange streaks illuminated the sky, exploding over the mountains.

She missed Chloe. She wanted to hold her tight, to sit here with her and watch the fish jump from the water as they caught the bugs hovering just above the surface and to snuggle under a warm blanket beside the fireplace.

She missed Jordan. What a fool she'd been, believing it was finally their time. How could she have believed he was different? She knew deep down she was being unfair to him. He was different. He was one of her best friends. It still hurt. It still made her angry, and she still felt betrayed.

She wished she could turn off her heart. Or at least the pieces left of it. In a matter of months her entire life had shifted, changed, and left her lost and off balance.

Pulling her feet from the water, she walked toward the cabin, letting the cold dew from the grass chill her bare feet, reminding her she could still feel something.

Once inside, she heated up a can of soup and ate it in front of the fire, staring blindly at the flames as they jumped and danced around the logs. She was used to being alone. She'd even come to enjoy it. But now, the silence sounded like screaming, the hours had stopped moving, and every movement she made felt like a puppet on a string.

Knocking the logs apart, she stirred the coals for more heat and placed the screen back across the fireplace before climbing under the heavy quilts and crying herself to sleep.

Chapter 27

Still no answer. Jordan fought the urge to throw his phone across the room and watch it shatter. Marissa had just vanished, and nobody knew where she'd gone. The only call she'd made was to Lexie to say she would be out of town for a few days and to cover her shift. This wasn't like Marissa at all, and he wasn't sure if he was worried or angry, but he was beginning to wear through his living room carpet.

He felt badly that he'd shouted at Lexie for not answering her phone at eleven o'clock at night, but he was upset no one had spoken to Marissa. Honestly, he was starting to get pissed off that she hadn't called him. He'd even broken a few laws by letting himself inside her house without a key, but he'd been concerned.

The knock on the door startled him, and he smacked his shin on the coffee table rushing to open it. He blurted out a couple of obscenities as the pain shot up his leg but made it to the door in a matter of seconds. His disappointment must have shown on his face as he opened the door for his sister.

"Nice to see you, too," Lexie snapped. "And nice mouth, Mom would've washed your mouth out with soap." She tossed her purse onto the kitchen counter. "I take it you haven't heard from her," she said, lowering herself slowly onto the couch. "Where in the hell did she go, and why did she just take off?" Without letting him answer, she turned and glared at him. "Did you do something? Did you two have a fight? I swear, Jordan Wayne, if you so much as—"

"No, we didn't have a fight," he interrupted.

Lexie leaned over and rested her head on his shoulder. "It doesn't make sense. She isn't the type of person to take off like that. She left me a message about work and disappeared." She turned to face him. "You don't think she's hurt or kidnapped or something, do you?"

Something didn't make sense. "Lex, did she tell you about Chloe?"

"What about Chloe?" It was obvious by the panic in her eyes she was clueless about what happened.

"The state came and picked up Chloe yesterday."

Her eyes grew large with a mixture of anger and confusion flashing in them. "Why? What do you mean picked her up? What does that mean, Jordan?"

"It seems Steven has a half-brother and he was granted temporary custody of Chloe," he informed her. He wished he wasn't always the bearer of bad news.

"He what?" Lexie tried to shoot off the couch, but seemed to give up the struggle and instead punched the cushion next to her. "Just who was Steven? Did he tell Marissa the truth about anything over the last eight years? A half-brother? Are they sure he really is?"

"It appears so," Jordan watched his sister's rage climb to the surface. Lexie was like a homicide waiting to happen.

"That coward!" she spat, finally pushing herself to her feet. "Hasn't he caused her enough pain? Now his secrets are ripping her daughter out of her arms." Her face had turned a deep shade of red; he was convinced there couldn't be any blood remaining in the rest of her body.

Jordan reached out and stopped her mid-stride. "We can scream about what a selfish ass Steven was later. Right now we have to find Marissa."

Chapter 28

Jordan hadn't slept more than two hours all night. His body demanded sleep, but his mind wouldn't cooperate. Where was she? It wasn't like her to leave without a word. She was the responsible one, the communicator, not the one to leave everyone who loved her sick with worry.

The sun wasn't up yet, but he needed to clear his head and convince his body to function at full capacity with no rest. Throwing on a pair of sweats and a t-shirt, he grabbed his iPod and headed to his favorite running trail.

The path was empty, dew still clung to the overhanging trees and the sounds of birds chirping surrounded him. He tucked his iPod away, deciding the sounds of nature would be his music of choice. The sun had just started to rise, leaving the trail barely visible. Having run the same trail for ten years, his autopilot was enough for him to continue without the light of day.

But he should have known nothing was going to lift the fog unless he knew Marissa was okay. He pictured her expression the night he'd told her about Steven and his betrayal, and the way her eyes were glazed over when she'd broken down and removed Steven's things from the house. The tears she'd cried when she learned Steven had another child with Jane, and her heartbreak of losing Annie and now Chloe. He was convinced it all been too much for her.

Even the strongest people crumbled sometimes, and he wanted to be there to help her smile again. He wasn't concerned she'd harm herself, but he was worried she could've been in an accident—or worse, had decided to simply run away from all of the painful memories. He knew logically she hadn't moved and left all of her belongings behind, nor would she leave her job and friends without proper notice, but his inability to make sense of her disappearing in the first place pushed him to think the worst.

Reaching the top of the trail, he paused to catch his breath. Suddenly he jerked upright, knowing exactly what he would do. Why hadn't he thought of it before? He turned and headed back toward town at a fast pace. He needed to get to the office. It was time to call in a favor.

• • •

Marissa woke to birds chirping and her teeth chattering. The fire had completely died out, and at some point she had kicked the quilt from the bed. Her head pounded and her eyes burned. She hadn't felt this bad in the morning since her high school reunion and an entire bottle of tequila.

Pulling the quilt around her shoulders, she started the fire again and walked into the tiny kitchen to make a pot of coffee. While she waited, she stepped out onto the porch and curled into the old wooden rocker to watch the sun rise.

A layer of fog hovered over the still lake, and dew glistened on the grass and trees surrounding her. It was peaceful here, but she knew she couldn't hide forever. She needed to learn how to live without Chloe in her life. She took a deep breath and blew it out slowly, refusing to allow herself to cry again.

She also needed to give up her silly, childish dreams of Jordan. He was now, and would always be, just her friend. If she ever forgave him, that is; she hoped they would continue to be friends. How was she supposed to turn off the feelings he stirred in her? Since they'd been intimate, something had changed for her.

Maybe changed wasn't the right word…resurfaced. She'd always felt something for Jordan, but after she'd met Steven she'd buried them and convinced herself it was a childhood crush. Once they'd moved back to Carmel, and Jordan became a part of her daily life again, it had become more difficult to keep her mind from wondering about him, them, the past, and the future. But she'd made a commitment to Steven, and she'd kept her vow to him.

She clenched her fist as the photograph of Steven standing beside another bride flashed through her mind. Who had she married? Had she ever really known him at all? It certainly didn't appear so. He'd made a fool of her.

He'd been her husband for eight years; it would be logical to miss him after his death. But she didn't. Maybe it was her anger, his betrayal, or the realization they were never meant to be together, but other than rage and humiliation, she didn't feel for him.

Every part of her, however, yearned for Chloe. She knew the last existing part of her heart had died as she watched the caseworker take Chloe away. Now she felt nothing but pain and grief. Her only moment of comfort was when she felt nothing at all.

Rising from the rocker, she wandered back inside and closed the door behind her. Deciding to skip the coffee, she threw another log on the fire and curled up on the bed. She would sleep, the best way to feel nothing at all, and that was all she wanted.

Chapter 29

She was tossing and turning and mumbling in her sleep, but Jordan resisted the urge to wake her. Her eyes were swollen, and black streaks of mascara lingered on her cheeks. Her hair was matted to her scalp, and she had the quilt wrapped tightly around her like a cocoon even with the overwhelming heat inside the small cabin. What was she doing in a secluded cabin close to the Oregon border?

He stepped outside, reminding himself that his goal had been to make sure Marissa was safe. He pulled his cell phone from his pocket and began to walk toward the clearing, searching for a signal.

"She's okay," he informed his sister.

"She's home? Where was she?" Lexie was talking so fast Jordan had to wait for her to finish before he could answer.

"She's not home. She is actually in a little cabin close to the state line. Don't hop in your car, Lex. I will talk to her. She's asleep and it looks like she needed it, so I'm waiting until she wakes up," he reassured her.

It was silent on her end of the phone for a moment and he wondered if he'd lost the signal. "How did you find her, Jordan?"

"I called in a favor and had her credit card activity pulled." He chuckled nervously. He knew his actions made him sound a bit crazy—after all, Marissa was a grown woman who'd only been gone for three days, but anyone who knew her would testify this was completely out of character for her even under the circumstances. Or at least that was how he'd justified his misuse of police resources.

Lexie exhaled loudly. "You're brilliant." He could hear the relief in her voice. "Promise you'll call me as soon as you talk to her. I won't be able to function until you do."

He promised and hung up the phone before returning to the cabin to wait.

• • •

Marissa awoke shivering and pulled her legs closer to her body and the quilt tighter.

"It's at least a hundred degrees in here."

She jumped, scooting to the head of the bed. Her heart raced as she tried to focus her eyes in the dim light. "Jordan? What are you doing here?"

"I've been worried sick." He stood from the chair in the corner and sat on the edge of the bed. "What are you doing all the way out here? Why didn't you tell somebody you were leaving?"

She bowed her head and tried to gather her thoughts. "I'm sorry I worried you. I told Lexie I'd be out for a few days," she said defensively.

Edging closer to her, he lifted her chin and forced her to look into his worry filled eyes. "Marissa, talk to me. Please let me in."

A sob ripped from her throat, and she started to cry and shake, leaning toward him, letting him hold her. She was surprised she had any tears left to shed, but it was clear she did. She couldn't form a word or pull herself together. She simply let Jordan rock her like a child while she sobbed in his arms.

It seemed like an eternity before she was able to speak, and the only word she could mumble was "water." He walked into the kitchen and came back with a tall glass of water and a handful of paper towels. He handed both to her and sat silently, giving her time to compose herself.

"How did you find me?"

He clenched his jaw, a sign she immediately recognized as frustration. "I'm a cop, it's what I do."

She waited for him to continue, but he sat silently rubbing her hand. "How could you do that to me, Jordan? How could you show up with Chloe's caseworker to take her away from me and not warn me, or give me a call first? Anything to let me know what was about to happen?" She wiped the tears that spilled down her cheeks.

"I couldn't. It was my job." He rubbed his eyes, his frustration apparent. "I only hoped my being there would've made it easier somehow instead of another officer going with her. She was so upset when she called me, and I knew how hard it would be for you. I tried to help and it backfired. I'm sorry."

"I get it's your job," her voice rose a notch. "But it's me; not just anyone, *me*." Her hands began to shake. She didn't know how to make him understand how much he'd hurt her. "Sometimes it's not the rules you break but the reasons you do. It's about doing the right thing for someone, not because it's allowed by the rules or your job, but simply because the person means more to you. I'm simply asking why you couldn't bend the rules a little and warn me my life was about to implode." She exhaled in frustration.

Jordan's eyes grew sad, almost resigned. "Sometimes you have to follow the rules even when you wish you didn't—even when you'd rather walk away than abide by a legality. Even when you know it will hurt someone you care about."

Frustration filled her and she wanted to lash out. "But it was me!" she shouted, leaping from the bed.

Jordan stood and pulled her into his arms. She pushed against his chest, struggling for release. He held on tighter and waited for her to stop fighting him as he whispered soothing sounds into her ear and rocked her again.

"I don't know how to live without her," she whimpered. "It hurts so much."

"We'll get her back," he said in the same soothing voice. "It's not over yet, and Chloe is your daughter even if the courts don't see that yet."

She clung to the small fray of hope he gave her, and held onto him tightly, afraid she would float away if he let go. Jordan scooped her up and pulled her onto his lap, rocking her and smoothing his hand over her hair like he used to do with Chloe. Burying her face against his neck she let go and cried until she ran out of tears.

"If anything happens to her, Jordan…"

"I won't let anything happen to Chloe."

She snuggled in closer and let herself melt into him. His lips met hers in comfort and passion. Her need for him increased and she deepened the kiss, parting his lips with her tongue, and raking her hands through his hair. He laid her down onto the rug, sending flashes of heat through her body as he peeled back her sweater and ran his hands along her bare stomach and over her breasts.

She called out his name, each syllable a plea for more. His lips pulled from hers, inching down the side of her neck, igniting a path of fire. She clumsily fought with his shirt, popping a few buttons in her fight to get to the skin beneath.

She scratched her nails gently down his back, and traced the skin below the waistline of his jeans. She arched, aching to feel his skin against her naked breasts. Jordan mumbled breathlessly, but his hands told her everything she couldn't hear.

Like the two fumbling teenagers they'd been their first time, both of them continued to struggle with buttons and zippers, bumping heads and noses in their need to touch, to feel.

As the fire danced across their naked skin, Marissa wrapped around him like a vine to a tree. Her need for him consumed her as she pleaded for relief from the ache he was creating. With his eyes locked on hers he gave her everything she'd asked for, and more.

...

He watched her as she slept beside him on the rug. The firelight played across her hair that lay like a silky sheet behind her. Careful not to wake her, he lightly brushed a tendril from her cheek, loving the feel of it against his fingers. She was still the most beautiful woman he'd ever seen. Her cheeks were rosy, her lashes like a fan against her cheeks. He smiled, noticing her spray of freckles were more prominent in the firelight. Her mouth was red and swollen from his kisses and puckered as if she lay in wait for more.

How did a man get over a woman like Marissa? How was he supposed to move on when his heart wouldn't budge? Steven had done a number on her. He'd never liked him. From the first time he'd been introduced to him something about him was off. Jordan thought it was merely a jealous reaction, but as time passed he realized it wasn't envy, but an immediate mistrust. Steven had never looked him in the eyes. And as a man—not to mention a cop—that was a clear sign Steven was hiding something. Not for the first time, he wished Marissa had seen through him before he'd ripped her heart out. His betrayal had hurt her pride, her heart, and left her questioning her own self-worth.

He stood up, making sure not to disturb her. He slipped on his jeans and padded into the kitchen to rummage through the fridge, returning with a plate of scrambled eggs and toast for each of them.

Sitting back down beside her, he gently kissed her lips to wake her. She stretched, her beautiful body moving against the blanket. He longed to touch her again. Smiling, she sat up, and reached for his shirt. His heart melted when, unable to button it, she blushed. "Sorry," she mumbled. He chuckled at her impish expression, and offered her a plate. "What, no mimosas?" she teased.

"My clothes are in shreds after you've had coffee, I'm not sure I can handle you with morning-after mimosas."

Grasping the front of his shirt and pulling it closed around her, her face grew red again.

Suddenly he wasn't sure he wanted to eat. Instead, he wanted to bury his hands in her tussled hair and pull what remained of his shirt from her warm body. He shook his head. Looking at her made his brain foggy and his body ignite into flames. He took a deep breath and forced himself to look up at her, trying to ignore the warm flesh exposed by missing buttons.

They needed to get back. He had to bring Chloe home to her. He wanted—no, he needed—to see her happy again.

"Eat up, we need to get on the road."

Chapter 30

Marissa hung up the phone and read the notes she'd written. Ms. Williams didn't know much about Steven's mysterious brother, only that he was older by four years, raised by his father, and he and Steven shared the same mother. His name was Jack Lowell and he'd been the one to contact child services asking about Chloe. He was married, had no children, and drove a garbage truck. None of this explained why Steven had never mentioned him to her.

A knock on the door interrupted her thoughts. The moment she'd opened the door for Lexie, her friend flew at her to wrap her in a tight hug.

"Who is this guy?" Lexie asked, walking into the kitchen and pouring herself a cup of coffee. "His brother? Seriously? And no one knew he existed before now?"

Relieved to be able to focus on facts and not her emotions, Marissa told Lexie everything she knew, which wasn't much.

"There has to be something, some clue, in Steven's belongings." Lexie plopped onto the stool beside her and read the notes with her. "A picture, a letter, a phone number, something."

Marissa shook her head and frowned. "There might have been, but I tossed everything into the street during my infamous rant. It's all been thrown away."

Lexie's eyes lit up. "No, it hasn't." She reached into her purse and pulled out her cell phone.

"What are you talking about?"

"When Dad came to help Jordan clean up your yard, they saved all the paperwork and files until you were emotionally ready to go through them." She scrolled and dialed. "Dad has it in boxes in the garage."

Marissa's heart raced as she listened to Lexie's end of the conversation. "Okay, see you soon," she said before hanging up.

"He's bringing it here?" she asked. "He doesn't have to do that. I can pick it up."

"Mom's cleaning the house," Lexie said with a chuckle. "Dad was begging for an excuse to run away. Trust me, there's no talking him out of it."

Marissa laughed.

"He made a terrific suggestion." Lexie sipped her coffee. "He said you should request any paperwork from his other...his other...crap, I don't know what to call it, but you should have any paperwork from his other house. If Jane doesn't have anyone and you were legally still his wife, you should be able to get ahold of that."

"I never thought of that. Of course he could have documents there." She picked up her cell phone and placed the call.

An hour later Jim Wayne left, grumbling and whining about how selfish they both were to not let him help. Neither had the heart to tell him his wife called and demanded his immediate return, insisting he wasn't going to get away from his share of the work.

The two of them sat cross-legged on the living room floor staring at the piles of boxes.

"Where the heck do we start?" Lexie blew out a breath.

"I suppose we each take a box and go."

Marissa lifted a box from the pile and set it in front of her, lifting the lid. She noticed some papers were torn and splattered with dirt. Clearly her destructive tirade was even messier than she'd remembered.

"Can I ask you something?" Lexie removed another lid.

"Like I've ever been able to stop you."

"Ha-ha, very funny. Seriously, how are things with you and Jordan?"

She wasn't sure how to respond. It was still too raw. "Jordan's been an amazing friend to me through this nightmare."

Lexie's hands dropped into her lap and she turned her head and scowled at her. "That's it? 'Jordan has been an amazing friend?'" She shook her head. "I'll pretend I don't know you've spent the night with him, or how I saw him leaving your room at Emily's party. I'll even forget for a minute you're my best friend and he's my brother. But I saw your face when Jordan showed up with Willow at the reunion. I was there when you disappeared and he couldn't find you. I saw the panic in his eyes and the lack of sleep. You two are much more than 'amazing friends' and you're both too damn stubborn to do something about it."

She was surprised by the annoyance in her friend's tone. "I don't understand why you're angry. Jordan and I are working through a few things, the main one being that he allowed me to be blindsided by the state when he knew they were coming to take away my daughter. Not a very more-than-friends move."

Lexie clucked her tongue. "You know he came with your caseworker because he thought it would make things easier for you, not because he was trying to hurt you."

"But he did hurt me," she snapped. "If he was worried about hurting me, he could have taken off his damn badge for a minute and called me with a warning. Instead he hid behind code and protocol, and it pisses me off."

"It's important to him," Lexie said gently. "His job, the rules he follows; it's a part of him."

"Well my daughter is a part of me." She didn't want her friend making excuses for what Jordan did. She wanted someone to understand why she was mad and tell her she had a right to be. She looked down, pretending to concentrate on the pile of papers in front of her. "Right now, the only thing I'm concerned with is getting Chloe back. I don't have time to contemplate the confusing relationship I have, or don't have, with your brother."

Lexie mumbled under her breath, but Marissa was able to make out something about too much wasted time.

"I don't want to fight with you, especially about this," she told her. "All I am sure of at this moment is I miss Chloe, and something in my gut tells me this Jack person isn't who he seems to be. I have to focus on getting her back, or at least making sure she's safe." She reached over and gripped her friend's hand. "I'm in no place emotionally to have a healthy relationship with anyone right now. I hope you can understand."

"So what exactly are we looking for?"

Marissa knew the storm had passed and Lexie was letting it go, this time. "Anything that will help us figure out who this guy is, and why Steven never mentioned he existed."

Chapter 31

Only three boxes remained and so far all Marissa had found were a few canceled checks written to Jack Lowell from Steven on an account she hadn't known about.

She sat the pile aside and rose to answer the door. Jordan stood on the porch in jeans and a t-shirt, his hair ruffled from the wind. He held a bag from her favorite Chinese food restaurant and a laptop computer. She tried to avoid looking at the muscles on his chest that moved when he did, or the way his sleeve rose just above his biceps. Now wasn't the time for her body to yearn for his touch, or for her own hands to long to travel beneath his shirt.

"Are you going to let me in?"

Marissa's head jerked up, and she felt the heat rising on her cheeks. She smiled nervously and opened the door for him.

"Lexie told me what you two had been doing this afternoon, and it got me thinking." He strolled into the kitchen and set the bag on the counter and the laptop next to it. "Steven traveled all the time for work, and people like that don't go anywhere without their laptop, right?" he continued, obviously not asking her the question. "So where was his? It had to have been in the car or his other house, because we didn't pick it up in the yard." He laughed.

She pursed her lips and tipped her head.

"Sorry," he smirked. "Well it seems with everything that happened, and the confusion with the two wives thing—"

"I take it you've found Steven's laptop?" she interrupted.

For a moment he seemed disappointed she'd stopped his story. She didn't want him to know how grateful she was. He wasn't off the hook for his behavior yet. "Yea, this is it. I thought you might find something in here that could help." He held out the computer.

"Thanks. I'm coming up short in the paperwork from his office with the exception of a few checks to this guy, Jack Lowell."

He walked around the counter and grabbed two plates from the cupboard. "I also knew you wouldn't have stopped long enough to eat something."

He was right, and the scent wafting through the kitchen had her stomach growling. She powered up the laptop and pushed it to the side to unload the cartons from the bag.

"Wine or water?"

"Water, please."

Jordan had not only stopped at her favorite Chinese restaurant—Steven wouldn't have paid enough attention to know that—but he'd brought her beef and broccoli ordered to her preferred spicy level. Her husband wouldn't have known those either. Was it because she spent more time with Jordan than she had her own husband? No, it was that both men were completely different. Jordan paid attention; he asked questions and listened to her answers. He remembered because he cared.

So then why had Jordan not known her well enough to understand her disappointment in the role he'd played the day they took her daughter? She knew he cared about her, and even believed he'd had the best intentions when he decided to be the one to come over with the caseworker, but he had to know how she'd react. How important it would've been to be forewarned what was about to happen.

She hadn't realized Jordan had been speaking to her until he waved his hand in front of her face.

"Are you okay?"

She smiled sheepishly. "Have a lot on my mind, sorry."

He dished them both up, and again she noticed he knew exactly what she liked. He handed her a napkin and a set of chopsticks and slid a glass of ice water next to her plate.

"His laptop is locked," he told her, moving it between them. "Any idea what his password might be?"

"Nope." She shook her head and rolled her eyes.

She tried his birthday, both wives' names, and his mother's maiden name. Nothing. She tried Chloe's name, and then her birthday.

"I'm in, it was Chloe's birthday," she said excitedly. "But what am I looking for?"

"Start with any correspondence or financial records. The same things we were looking for in the boxes for the most part."

We? She looked at him confused for a moment, but as he dug his chopsticks into the carton, she realized he must have been referring to her and Lexie.

She searched Jack's name and came up empty. Most of the files on this laptop were work related.

"Go through the browser history," Jordan instructed. "See if you can locate an email account."

She did as instructed and was grateful to discover Steven had saved it so no password was required. She'd always used his work email, and she'd been unaware he had another one, although at this point, nothing about Steven would shock her.

Scanning through the inbox, she saw nothing unusual. Opening the sent file, she slowly skimmed through, reading the names of the addressees. She stopped when she saw a reply sent to a Four-Jacks email address. She knew it was Steven's brother.

"I found something, listen to this." She moved down to the original message from Jack. "Steven, I need your help. This is the last time, I swear."

"What was Steven's response?"

"I'm done. I told you never again and I meant it. You're on your own. Please don't contact me in the future." She rested her chin on her hand and read it to herself again. "What do you think this was all about?"

"I have no idea. What's the date on it?"

She went back to the top. "It was a month before Steven's accident."

"Is there anything else?"

She forwarded the email to her own account, just in case, and started searching again. Finding nothing, she went to the top to go through the list one more time. Nothing else from Jack, but one address caught her attention and she opened it.

Forgetting she wasn't alone, she read the lengthy email to herself, cursed aloud, and read it again. She slammed the laptop closed and cursed again.

"What is it?" Jordan asked, surprising her.

"That woman!" she seethed.

She desperately wanted to break something. She needed to move. Jumping up from the stool, she picked up the dishes and headed to the sink. "What kind of..."

Jordan tipped his head, his brow creased in confusion. "What kind of what? What woman?"

"That miserable, scheming, greedy..."

"Marissa," Jordan raised his voice impatiently. "Please stop talking to yourself and talk to me. What did you find?"

Whipping around, she glared at him. "Who do you think? That so called 'innocent other woman,' Jane, was not innocent in the slightest!" Her voice rose and fury blazed through her as she fought for control.

"What do you mean?" he asked carefully.

"She knew he was married," she raged. "She knew about me."

Jordan raised his eyebrow. "She knew he was married to you, but married him anyway?"

"Yes. No," Marissa growled in frustration. "She found out right after Chloe was born. According to her email, she originally thought he was having a fling with me."

Jordan appeared confused. "Who was this email to? I'm struggling to understand here."

"The email was to Steven." She slammed the dishwasher closed and wrung the kitchen towel in her hands. "She told him he had to choose between us, and within five minutes, he'd replied, begging her not to leave him."

Jordan's jaw clenched and his eyes darkened. "Are you telling me you're angry because Steven chose her? You've known that for months now."

"No, even if he were alive I wouldn't want him! They can have each other!"

"Then why are you so angry?"

"Because she was a manipulative bitch!" Marissa threw the towel down on the counter. "She discovered I was up for a promotion at work. I don't know how, but she did. She actually told him to wait to leave me until I'd received it so I couldn't come at him for any of his income." She paced, furious beyond her own comprehension. "Oh, and of course, requested he didn't sleep with me. Ha! Like that was an issue." Picking up the dish rag, she wiped the counter again. "Who the hell does that?"

"But it never became a money issue—"

"That's not the point!" Marissa slammed her hand against the counter. "What kind of hateful, cold blooded, selfish, greedy…" She forced herself to take a breath and exhale. "There's a natural decency in people—or at least most people—where there'd be a moment of sympathy for the other woman who's being betrayed and doesn't know it. She wants to keep him around knowing he's a lying coward, fine, but her first thought was to screw me over. Not 'you have to tell her, it's the right thing to do,' but 'hey, if we wait a little while I can have all your big man executive money.' What kind of woman does that?"

Without waiting for a response she continued, "I never met her, but by that email I can tell you she had no soul; no heart. She was as cold as her condo. It boggles my mind how two people as horrible as Steven and Jane could have possibly produce a child as wonderful and loving as Chloe."

Jordan sat in silence, his face an emotionless mask.

"You think I'm crazy to be upset over this, don't you?"

He shook his head. "I don't think you're crazy. But I do have to wonder if that's the real reason you're so angry."

"What other reason would there be?" she snarled. "Isn't that reason enough? Whose side are you on? It certainly seems it's not mine."

"Of course I'm on your side, and I'm not saying you don't have reason to be angry. I'm just saying your reason for being furious might be something for you to seriously think about. Maybe you haven't gotten past Steven's betrayal as you insist you have. Or maybe you loved him more than you let on, and you're jealous he picked Jane over you. I know how badly it hurts. It takes a very long time to get past it."

She knew he was talking about her choosing Steven over him. She knew that was how he saw things then. But worse, she worried he might be right. Was she this angry because Jane broke the unspoken girl code, or because Steven wanted Jane and was willing to leave her with nothing after all the years they'd spent together?

Jordan stood up and started straightening her notes. "I'm gonna get going. Let me know if you find anything useful regarding Jack and if I can do anything to help." He leaned over, kissed her on the cheek, and walked out.

The door closing behind him echoed through the quiet house. Well, she supposed that was one way to let him go and save her heart from the pain she feared the most. So why did it hurt?

Chapter 32

Jordan wasn't ready to go home. He was angry and frustrated and had driven around for a couple of hours trying to clear his head. In his opinion, Steven had committed the worst sin imaginable, and still Marissa seemed as if she were trying to make some sense of it. So what if the other woman was a conniving opportunist? It served Steven right to be married to someone like her after all he'd put Marissa through.

He pulled into the full parking lot of the local tavern. He wanted to have a cold beer and get lost in the noise of the old jukebox and the basketball fans sure to be cheering for the Lakers. Opening the door, he was instantly overwhelmed by the smell of beer and sweat. People shouted out in welcome as he made his way around the pool tables and numerous bodies, his eye on the last stool open at the bar. He ordered a draft and pretended to focus on the game playing on the television above the bar, but his mind was filled with Marissa.

She claimed she hadn't been in love with Steven for years, so why did he wonder how true that really was? He wanted to shake her and scream, "I'm right here," but he also knew it wouldn't do any good. She continued to pull away. He was no longer sure if her reasoning had to do with Steven and her obvious lack of trust with the male gender, or if she was actually grieving his death.

Maybe this all stemmed from her loss of Chloe. He'd like to believe that was the case. Maybe she was simply protecting herself from any more pain or loss. If she was still this upset about his presence when her caseworker had taken Chloe, he had little hope she'd forgive him if she learned the rest of what he was keeping from her.

He knew exactly who had rolled up to stand beside him before he even looked. Her scent was distinct and the sound of her purr as she casually glided her foot along his leg was unmistakable.

Jerking his leg out of reach, he turned and glared at her. "Willow, what are you doing here?"

"I came to get out for a bit and was pleasantly surprised to see you sitting here all alone." Her eyes filled with longing.

"I came here to be alone," he informed her, hoping she'd take the hint.

"Jordan, I'm a great listener. You look like you could use a friend right now." She reached over and ran her hands through his hair.

He gripped her hand and pulled it back down to the bar. "Willow, nothing is going to happen between us. I think I made myself clear on this subject."

It was suddenly obvious that being turned away was not something she was familiar with. Her expression was filled with shock, and a slight flash of challenge.

"You and I had dinner a few times. That's it," he tried to explain. "I told you we were only friends from the day I ran into you and every time I saw you after, so I never led you on."

"It's Marissa, isn't it?" She bit off each word. "It's always been Marissa."

It was Marissa, but he wasn't about to open that old wound. He wasn't in the mood for one of Willow's famous rants.

"We're friends, Willow." He took a sip of his beer. "And I don't want to be rude, but I've had a crappy day and I just want to be alone."

Jordan sighed as she snapped her purse over her shoulder and marched from the bar. Of all people, she was the last one he wanted to see. He wanted to be alone. He needed time to figure out how to get himself untangled from this rope that was tightening around his neck with every step Marissa took closer to the mysterious half-brother, Jack Lowell.

Chapter 33

Marissa sat on Chloe's bed and hugged a fluffy, white teddy bear to her chest. She missed her so much. The sound of her laughter, the sweet way she held her arms out for a kiss goodnight, and the expression on her face when she came down the slide in the backyard. Even though they'd only been together a few months, Chloe had become a permanent part of her life, and she couldn't imagine another day without her.

Tears rolled down her cheeks as she propped the teddy bear back against the pillow. She walked over to the closet and opened the door. The small hangers were mostly empty, and the few remaining items were one size too large for Chloe. She'd been growing so fast, Marissa decided to be prepared. She wondered if they'd fit her now.

Closing the closet doors, she turned to leave, stopping at her daughter's dresser to pick up the ballerina figurine Ryan had given Chloe as a welcome gift. She imagined those two would have grown up to be best friends. Ryan was so protective of her, always worried she'd get hurt. He must have learned that from his Uncle Jordan.

She set the figurine back, bumping the picture of Steven's parents she'd brought back from his home in Los Angeles. It fell to the floor, shattering the glass. She was relieved none of the broken glass had scratched the picture. She removed the back from the frame and pulled the picture out. With it fell a key.

It looked to be some sort of a safe deposit box key. But from where, and why did Steven have the key hidden? This whole situation continued to get more and more frustrating.

After cleaning up the broken glass and slipping the key into her wallet, she made a list of all of the banks in the area that offered safe deposit boxes. She'd have go to each one and see if she could find this mysterious box.

By four o'clock, Marissa had been to every bank within twenty miles and none of them had a safe deposit box for Steven Neil. It wasn't until she'd climbed into the bathtub that she realized the picture had been at his other house. It would be logical the bank would be in Los Angeles.

She quickly rose from the bathtub, dried, dressed, and made a reservation on the next flight out. Within forty-five minutes, she was packed and climbing into a taxi to take her to the airport.

By the time she'd landed and picked up her rental car, she was exhausted. She checked into the hotel, ordered a light dinner, and was fast asleep before midnight.

When the phone rang as her wakeup call the following morning, she called Lexie to tell her where she was and save herself the lengthy lectures for worrying her friend.

There were too many banks in the area to visit all of them. She decided to start with the bank the check to Jack was drawn on. There she approached the first available teller—Kym with a Y— and told her what she was looking for. Kym excused herself and came back moments later with the branch manager.

And just like that, Marissa had found it. John, the branch manager, asked for the paperwork, and she handed him the death certificate, as well as their marriage license. She was glad she hadn't run it through the shredder in the den, because she'd contemplated it many times.

They walked through a locked door, and she handed John the key from her purse. He turned it and his key simultaneously, pulled out the box, and set it on the counter for her before leaving her alone.

Her hands shook as she opened the lid. Taking a deep breath, she let it out slowly and took the first envelope from the box. Unfolding the paper inside, she realized it was Steven's marriage license to Jane. Her stomach turned as she stared at his signature on the page. How dare him. How dare he treat her like she was disposable, like he hadn't already made a commitment and wasn't free to do so again.

The next envelope contained Chloe's birth certificate. Behind that, a legally filed will stating Chloe was to receive all of his assets. Reading further down, she finally found the proof she needed. She'd been listed as requested guardian if Jane were unavailable or deceased. Hugging the form against her chest, she couldn't help but smile. She tucked it into her purse and returned to the next item in the box.

It was a childhood picture of Steven standing beside a young, sandy-haired boy with a missing front tooth and a pretty little blonde girl with her hair in braids, clinging to Steven like she worried he might fly away. Turning the picture over it read, Steven, Jack, and Laura. It appeared Jack did exist, but who was Laura?

The box contained another photo of an older Jack sitting at a poker table with a frown on his face. Pulling the picture closer, she could see the perspiration on his forehead. So much for Jack having a poker face—or whatever the term was. It was obvious he was holding a losing hand.

The next picture was mostly the same, only at a different location and sitting beside an older gray-haired man who seemed to be in the same sinking ship as Jack. There was a photo of Jack entering a casino, Jack leaving a casino, and one of him at the cashier's cage. In another picture he stood in a parking lot, but she could see a part of the sign in the background and it appeared to be a casino as well. In this picture Jack was handing something to an unkempt young man, not much older than twenty she guessed. She couldn't see what Jack was handing him, but both of them looked like they were watching for someone.

Why did Steven have pictures of Jack gambling and standing in a parking lot of a casino? It appeared Jack didn't know the photos were being taken. It was like someone was following him and documenting what he did. But why? She put the stack of photos in her purse as well and reached back into the box.

None of this was making any sense. She didn't understand why Steven would have these items locked up in a safe deposit box, or how any of this was tied to Jack, or even if it was. The only item left in the box was a business card of a police officer named Jeffery Hamilton. Well she knew where she needed to start if nothing else. She took all the contents with her, replaced the box, and drove back to the hotel.

Chapter 34

The next morning, Marissa walked into the police station listed on the card and asked to see Jeffery Hamilton. They pointed her to a waiting room to the left of the reception area and she sat in a bright orange, cracked vinyl chair to wait. Fifteen minutes later, Jeffery Hamilton introduced himself. She wasn't sure what she expected, but it wasn't the man who shook her hand. He wore a short-sleeved, button-up shirt with a spot of coffee on the front. The khaki pants he wore were wrinkled and about three inches too short. He had thinning, gray hair, a five o'clock shadow at ten in the morning, and a habit of constantly pushing his horn rimmed glasses back onto his nose.

"What can I do for you, Ms. Neil?" The smile he'd worn when he held out his hand suddenly vanished and his thick brows drew down, creating a perfect V shape across his forehead. "Neil? Have we met before?"

"No, we haven't." She held the card out to him. "I found this in a safe deposit box belonging to my husband. I was wondering how you knew him?"

"Your husband?"

"Yes, Steven Neil."

It was evident by the look on his face he knew who she was talking about. "You said you're his wife?"

Unable to stop herself, she laughed. It was far from funny, but it beat crying about it, she supposed. "It seems I was one of two."

He looked confused but didn't ask her to elaborate. Instead he asked, "He didn't tell you how he came to have my card?"

"No. I found it after he passed away."

His brows drew together again, and he wiped his hands against his thighs. "Come into my office."

It was more a demand than a request as he quickly turned and led her through the secured door and down a long hallway. He held the door open for her, and closed it securely behind them. Gesturing to a burgundy vinyl chair for her, he sat at his desk and ran his hands through what remained of his hair.

"Steven is dead?"

"So you did know him?"

"I did. He came to me with questions regarding a case I was involved in." He quickly closed his mouth and clenched his lips together like he'd said too much. "You said you were his wife? One of two?"

She pulled out her marriage license and handed him the one she'd found showing Steven's marriage to Jane. "She passed away with him. That's how I found out about her."

He studied the papers in his hands before he let out a low whistle and handed the papers back to her. "How did they die?"

"In a car accident, why?" The hairs on the back of her neck stood up. "What case was he asking you about?"

"I'm not at liberty to discuss that with you. The case is still pending."

"Did you know Steven had a daughter?" she asked, trying not to overreact to the situation.

"I did." His eyes grew large. "She's okay, isn't she?"

Marissa frowned. "She's fine, she wasn't in the car. Please Mr. Hamilton, tell me what is going on."

"I wish I could. Tell me what brought you to see me."

"Someone is fighting me for custody of Chloe, Steven's daughter." She felt the heat climb up her cheeks. "I didn't know he had a daughter or another wife, and now I've discovered a long lost brother. None of this is making any sense."

He jumped up from his chair and began to nervously pace the room. "Brother?" His face had grown completely white.

She stood up, too; her heart felt like it was going to beat out of her chest. Something was seriously wrong. "Yes, his name is Jack Lowell. Does this case have anything to do with him?"

Sympathy filled his eyes. "I wish I could help you, I honestly do, but my hands are tied on this." He opened the door for her.

"This is an innocent little girl we're talking about," she said firmly. "Is she in danger?"

"I hope not," he said, and closed the door, leaving Marissa standing with her mouth agape on the other side.

• • •

Jordan picked up his phone, studying the file in front of him without noting the caller ID. "Wayne."

"Jordan, it's Scott."

His head jerked up. "Everything okay?"

"I'm not sure," he said honestly. "Marissa was in here today."

"What do you mean she was in there? She's in LA?"

"Yeah, and she met with Hamilton, and now he seems really flustered."

"Hamilton?" Jordan stood, his pulse racing when Scott confirmed. "Do you know why she went to see him?"

"No idea. He closed his door the minute she entered." Scott, his friend, replied. "I was surprised to see her and concerned when I saw the look on Hamilton's face as he blazed out of here the moment she left. I thought you were going to keep her out of this."

Yeah, right. Keeping Marissa out of this when her mama bear claws were out was going to be impossible. Instead, he'd do what he could to keep her safe.

"I've got to give her something, Scott. I know this is bigger than a custody case for you, but this is her daughter we're talking about and she's not going to stop until she brings her home." He was suddenly feeling that he was drowning in all of these secrets.

Scott was silent on the other end of the phone. "Alright, Wayne, give her a copy of his rap sheet. Maybe that will help."

"Thanks, man, I'll be there on the next flight out. Let me know if you see her with Hamilton again."

He hung up the phone, picked it up again and dialed his sister. "Lexie, I need to know where to find Marissa. It's important."

Chapter 35

Jordan noticed her surprise when Marissa opened the door to see him standing in the hallway. "You should never open the door without asking who it is. Safety 101."

"What are you doing here?" she asked, opening the door wider for him.

"I'm worried about you. You're out in Los Angeles playing Nancy Drew alone."

Marissa narrowed her eyes. "I'm a big girl, Jordan. I'm just trying to find out about Jack Lowell and why there is so much secrecy regarding him. He has my daughter, you don't think I'm just going to sit back and do nothing?"

He sighed. "No, I know you won't do that. But I don't want you running all over LA by yourself. At least let me help you."

"I don't need a babysitter," she said defiantly.

"I'm not here to babysit you, Marissa. I'm here to help if you'll let me."

Her eyes drew together. "How did you know I was here?"

Crap, he hadn't thought this part through. "I have a friend who recognized you and let me know he'd seen you."

She narrowed her eyes. "A friend? And how would they know me?"

"That isn't the point," he snapped.

"Really?" she said suspiciously. "You get a call from someone I've never met but who knows me and feels inclined to inform you I'm in town. What is really going on, Jordan?"

"Nothing," he stammered.

She rose from the bed and placed her hand on her hip. "Don't walk in here telling me you're here to help and then lie to me. I've had enough dishonesty in the last few months to last me a lifetime."

Every part of him wanted to spill all he knew. But protocol wouldn't allow it, and if he didn't convince her he was clueless, she was going to run into this mess head first and blind.

"Marissa, he's a friend of mine from the police academy. And if you're going to make me say it, he recognized you because he was the friend I got drunk with years ago when you married Steven, and in a moment I'm not proud of, might've pulled your picture out to whine over. Now that I'm completely humiliated, can we move on from the twenty questions?"

Marissa chuckled. "Why didn't you just say so?"

He rose from the bed to answer the second knock at the door. "Are you expecting someone?" His nerves were suddenly on edge.

"Room service."

He opened the door and waited as the bell boy wheeled in the cart and lifted the lids from her meal.

"I have plenty here, are you hungry?" she asked him.

"No, thank you, I grabbed a bite at the airport." He sat back down beside her. "I take it you found something about Jack?"

She nodded and swallowed the bite of salad she'd been chewing. Moving over to the desk, she picked up the stack of items she'd removed from the safe deposit box and set them on the bed between them.

"It doesn't make sense to me," she told him. "There are all these pictures of who I assume is Jack sitting at a poker table, or a cashier's window at a casino, in a parking lot talking to some young man. It looks like private eye stuff." She handed him the stack of pictures.

"That's exactly what it is." He picked through the photos and studied each one again.

"Did Hamilton give you any insight as to what was going on with Steven?"

"How did you know about Hamilton?" She shook her head and frowned. "Never mind. And no, he didn't tell me anything, although he became very agitated when I mentioned Jack."

Jordan tried to put the pieces into some sort of logical order. He picked up each photo again, and set them down like he was assembling a jigsaw puzzle. "I asked him if Chloe could be in danger and his response worried me a little."

Jordan felt his pulse increase. "What *exactly* did he say?"

"He said he hoped not."

He clenched his jaw. "What in the hell does that mean?"

"I don't know." She reached down and picked up the will. "But I think I have the key to get her out of here and bring her home."

"What is it?"

"Steven legally filed a will listing me as his requested guardian for Chloe."

"Finally, some good news." He knew it wouldn't be as easy as presenting Steven's will, but it was a step in the right direction. "And speaking of good news..."

He handed her the file he'd brought with him.

She opened it, scanning the pages, her brow knit in concentration. "Possession with intent to sell? He's a drug dealer?"

"He was charged but got off by a technicality."

"But it can help us, right?"

"We need to find a lawyer, but yes, I think it's worth a shot."

She smiled and threw her arms around him, squeezing him with excitement.

Chapter 36

Marissa was surprised to see Chloe's caseworker waiting in the reception area of the lawyer she'd recommended.

"I hope it's okay that I'm here," she said sheepishly. "I just feel so responsible for this case. I can't stop thinking about it."

Marissa wrapped her arms around the caseworker. "I'm really glad you're here, Ms. Williams."

"Please, after all of this, call me Diane."

Within five minutes she, Jordan, and Diane were seated in the office of Caroline Dean. The attorney was a tall, thin woman with her salt-and-pepper hair cut short against her scalp, and her smile filled her cocoa brown face with perfectly white teeth. Marissa liked her instantly.

After shaking Marissa's hand, she sat back at her desk and slipped on a pair of glasses. "I've reviewed your file, and I believe we have a case here. The legal will is not a guarantee of guardianship, but it will weigh heavily in your favor," she informed them. "Also, I believe his arrest will cast a shadow, but could easily be dismissed because he wasn't convicted. The final decision will still be the judge, but it looks good. There are, however, a few things I should mention that will work against you." She looked pointedly at Marissa. "One is your single status, but as your husband of record has just recently passed, we can argue that. If Mr. Lowell gets a good lawyer, they'll argue that Chloe is your husband's illegitimate child and you therefore might have some resentment toward her."

"But that's not true!" she protested.

"It doesn't have to be true for it to be a point in their favor. It's obvious to me how much you love Chloe, and I believe the court will see that as well, but it's my job to inform you what you could be up against."

Jordan reached over and grasped her hand in support.

"The other point they're going to make is the blood relation," Ms. Dean continued. If Mr. Lowell is in fact Steven's half-brother, that is another point in their favor versus Steven's will. For now, we'll go with the assumption Mr. Lowell is Steven's blood relative because the courts removed Chloe from your home so quickly. I've sent for the records to verify this information myself." The lawyer sighed, removed her glasses, and leaned forward. "I can't begin to imagine what you've been through with all you've learned about your husband, but I have to ask, do you have any idea why Steven may have kept the fact he has a brother from you?"

Marissa's eyes filled with tears.

Ms. Dean reached across the desk and handed her a tissue, her face conveying sympathy.

Hell, she couldn't explain anything Steven had done over the years. Jordan was still holding her hand, lending her quiet support. She couldn't find it in herself to squeeze his fingers in return. Not yet.

"No, I don't. He was giving him money, and I found some strange pictures of who I think is Jack in a safe deposit box."

"Strange pictures?" Diane asked curiously.

"Well they're pictures of Jack playing poker and at casinos. It looks like they were taken without his knowledge. Jordan and I believe they were taken by a private investigator."

"That is odd," Ms. Dean agreed. "We might want to run our own investigation on Jack Lowell, but in the meantime I'll file a notice for a new hearing based on the discovery and request a rush due to mitigating circumstances. With you currently in Los Angeles, and the importance of the parental request, I don't believe we'll be denied the hearing. If you could, please stay in town a few more days and I'll contact you as soon as I hear back from the courts. I'll do whatever it takes to get your daughter back." She smiled at her with reassurance. "Just try to be patient."

Marissa choked back the lump that formed in her throat and mouthed, "Thank you."

Chapter 37

"I'm trying to be patient," Marissa said, wiping the tears from her cheeks.

She'd gone over the conversation in her mind the entire drive back to the hotel. The more she replayed it, the more it seemed like an impossible battle. Even the positive attitude the lawyer portrayed suddenly seemed half-hearted.

Jordan sat beside her on the bed, stroking her hand in his in silent support. She was glad he was here with her. She didn't think she could go through this alone.

• • •

"It hurts," she whimpered. "I can't stand it."

She lifted her head, her pain-filled eyes begging him for help. He was startled when she scooted closer to him and pressed her lips to his. Her kisses grew urgent, as she ran her hands through his hair and held his lips tightly against hers.

He moaned with need but pulled back hesitantly. Lifting her chin he gazed into her half closed eyes and saw the desire in their amber depths. Burying his hands in her hair, he laid her back on the bed and crushed his mouth to hers. The tip of his tongue slipped into the warm depths of her mouth, dancing against her tongue.

Her body arched off the bed, as she ran her hands beneath his t-shirt lightly scratching against his bare chest. Her primal groan sent shock waves through his system.

In the back of his mind he knew she was hurting, that she needed comfort not sex, but the writhing, demanding woman beneath him was looking for an escape, and his body quickly took over. Her hands were everywhere, tugging at his shirt, unbuckling his belt, and tugging on his zipper. They moved to her own clothes, popping buttons from her blouse, as she cried out in obvious need and frustration.

Part of him knew he should stop. But the thought this might be the last time he would be able to show her how he felt was consuming him. It wouldn't be long before he'd have to tell her what he'd known, and chance losing her again. He needed her, and she needed him. If only one last time.

Unable to control himself, he rolled onto his knees and pulled his shirt over his head, and finished removing his jeans. Without thought or logic, he grabbed the front of her blouse and pulled it apart, ripping off the remaining buttons to get to the warm flesh beneath. He made quick work on the snap of her bra and tearing it from her with one hand, used his other to knead her exposed breast.

Reaching behind his neck she pulled him down, her back arching, directing his mouth to her breast. "Jordan," she called out. He suckled her nipple, first one, than the other, her moans and demands for more pushed him to the brink. Sucking her nipple between his teeth, he lightly bit, and rolled his tongue over the taunt bud.

It'd never been like this before, not with Marissa, not with anyone, and he felt he might die from need. She shouted his name, crying out for release, her nails digging into his back as he entered her. He met each of her thrusts, as she called out his name over and over again before he brought them each to climax and collapsed in her arms.

Chapter 38

When Marissa opened her eyes hours later, the room was dark. She stood up and looked out the window, seeing the sun had set hours earlier. How long had she slept? Picking up her cell phone and what was left of her blouse, she tiptoed into the bathroom attempting to not wake Jordan, and closed the door before turning on the light.

It was after ten and she'd missed a call from Lexie, but there were no other voicemails. Turning on the shower, she glanced in the mirror. Her eyes were bloodshot, her skin blotchy from crying. She had bruises forming in little circles on her shoulders and her thighs.

What had gotten into her? She'd attacked him like he was water and she'd been in the desert for years. She'd wanted him so badly, the pain was physical, like nothing she'd ever felt before. Part of her wanted to regret it. She was so confused about how she felt about Jordan. One minute she was convinced he was the man she was destined to be with, the next, someone who would always put his job before her. She never wanted that in her life again after her years with Steven. Or was she merely overreacting because she'd been emotionally drained over the last few months?

At times she thought she'd be doing him a favor if she were to let him go. The baggage she was carrying around was heavy for any man, no matter how much he looked capable of handling the weight. But something kept pulling her back to Jordan.

She'd needed him, wanted him, and after last night, would always crave him. But, she had to let him go. Didn't she? His job would always come first; he'd made that clear. So if they continued to build on a relationship more than friendship, wouldn't they lose it all when he chose his job over her again? Wasn't being with him now telling him she's okay to be in second place? If she had to choose between being his friend or not having him in her life, she'd immediately choose their friendship. But could they have both?

She was driving herself crazy with all the thoughts tumbling in her head. For now, she needed to concentrate on Chloe. Contemplating the rest of her life and Jordan's place in it was going to have to wait.

Climbing into the shower, she let the hot water run over her, soothing her sore muscles. She gasped when the shower door opened and her hand flew to her chest. "Jordan, you scared me to death."

"Were you expecting someone else?" he teased.

She laughed, but she could hear the nervousness in her own voice. "I was just getting out, it's all yours," she said, stepping past him.

He grabbed her around the waist, his warm lips kissing her neck, and his hands running gently over her breasts and down her stomach. "What's the rush? I just got here."

She placed her hand over his, stopping its decent, and without turning around said, "I'm sorry, Jordan, I can't do this right now. I need to focus on getting Chloe back. You understand, don't you?"

He said nothing at first but studied her face intently. She watched his eyes darken and noticed his stance change, almost as if he'd been deflated. "Yes, I think I do understand," he said and stepped into the spray of the shower.

Chapter 39

Marissa unlocked her front door and set her suitcase inside the foyer. Instantly, she feared the deafening sound of silence would remain. How would she ever win custody of Chloe when the courts found no fault with a criminal record, or seemed to care what the father wanted for his child? Even her lawyer had been surprised that a new hearing had been denied. She was down to one last chance. If she didn't win the actual custody hearing she would never be able to bring Chloe home.

She hadn't yet closed the door when there was a knock.

"Hellllo, Marissa, it's Dora, from next door," a female announced in a singsong voice.

Marissa plastered a smile on her face. "Hello, Dora, what can I do for you?"

"I've been waiting for you to come home for a couple of days. The postman left a large package for you. I signed for it, I hope that's okay. I told him you were out of town."

"Thank you," Marissa held out her hand for the large envelope her neighbor held clasped to her chest.

Without releasing the package, Dora continued, "I told him I didn't know how long you'd be gone, and it would be best to save you a trip into the post office."

"Thank you," Marissa repeated.

"I hope that's alright. I didn't know where you'd run off to, but I thought you wouldn't mind."

She could feel her patience waning. She clenched her jaw and took a deep breath. "Thank you, Dora." She reached out and yanked the package from her grasp. "I really appreciate your bringing it over," Marissa said as she quickly closed the door.

She knew she'd been rude, but her nosy neighbor was the last thing she wanted to deal with today. She set the package down and went upstairs to change and unpack. After starting a load of laundry, she poured herself a glass of wine and sat down to open the package.

She ripped open the manila envelope and lifted the stack of papers from inside. There was a form letter from Steven's office stating the personal papers belonging to Steven Neil were enclosed per her request, as was a flash drive discovered in his desk that did not contain company information. She'd actually forgotten she'd asked for them to be sent to her.

She carefully reviewed each one of the papers and found nothing pertaining to Jack, Chloe, or her. She picked up the flash drive, walked into the kitchen, and opened her laptop. Her eyes were drawn automatically to a file titled *My eyes only* and she immediately opened it.

The file contained copies of emails between Steven and Jack. She read through them, trying to understand the context. Jack wanted—no, the term he used most often was "needed"—money. Steven continued to tell him he wouldn't give him anymore because he hadn't learned to stay out of the same bad situations. What situations? Did this have to do with his possession charge?

Most of the emails were of the same, until she read the last one. Steven mentioned their sister. So was the blonde in the picture another sibling? And why had Marissa been kept in the dark about her as well? Without another thought, she opened her Bing search engine and typed in Laura Neil. Nothing came up. Then she typed in Laura Lowell, still nothing. How had Steven had two siblings his wife knew nothing about? Why would he keep them a secret? Why had he told her he was an only child? It didn't make any sense.

She wanted to call Jordan to get his thoughts on the emails. Why, when she chose to take a stand, did she always wish she hadn't? Jordan was her friend. If she called him, he'd come running. But she'd gotten tangled in their relationship again, and pushed him away. Worse, she'd hurt him. She wished she knew why she kept doing that.

She pulled out the envelope from the safe deposit box and stared at the same pictures again. She felt she was missing something every time she looked through them. Why did Steven have these pictures?

She fought the tears welling up as the silence cut through her. She missed Chloe.

She tucked the pictures back into the envelope before walking outside to check her mail. The mailbox was full—not surprising after having been gone for a week—but she hadn't the energy to deal with it. Instead, she laid it on the counter and headed to the living room to take a nap on the couch. She picked up Chloe's stuffed ladybug tucked inside a blanket and pulled it to her chest. Covering herself, she allowed the tears to fall.

When she woke, the sun had set, leaving the house cloaked in shadow as she reached for the light switch. She checked her phone, hoping Jordan had called but not surprised he hadn't.

She made a cup of tea and sat at the counter to go through her mail. Organizing it into piles, she thought again of taking Steven's old den and making it into an office for herself. It'd certainly clear the clutter from her kitchen.

Coming upon a small manila envelope, she turned it over to see who it was from. It hadn't gone through the mail, and there was no return address. It simply had her name written on the front above the word *Confidential*. With shaky hands, she cut through the seal. Inside were more photographs of Jack Lowell. This time he wasn't at a casino or a poker table but behind a building of some sort talking to the gray-haired man from the poker table at the casino. She couldn't make out what it was, but Jack was handing him something. The pictures appeared to be taken in the same style as the others, from farther away and seeming to be without his knowledge. She set the pictures aside and removed a typed note.

Jack Lowell has a sealed juvenile record that will help you.

There was no name; no hint as to who left the envelope or why they were warning her. She needed to call Jordan. This situation was getting weird. She picked up a stack of mail and walked into the den to leave it on the desk. Flipping on the light, the mail dropped from her grasp, her hand flew up to her chest and she struggled to catch her breath.

The entire room was ripped apart. All of the boxes she'd meticulously gone through had been dumped out and scattered. Every drawer was pulled open, and every filing cabinet tipped over.

Her heart beat fast. Her hands were sweating as she dialed 9-1-1. She returned to the kitchen, grabbed a knife, and stood in the corner, waiting for them to answer.

In less than five minutes, Jordan pulled into the driveway, sirens blasting through the silence, red and blue lights flashing through the kitchen window, creating a light show. She raced to the door and threw herself into his arms.

"Easy now." He pulled the knife from her white-knuckled grip. "It's okay, I'm here now."

She hadn't realized she'd been crying until he wiped her cheek. "I was so scared."

"Show me what you found," he instructed gently.

She walked him to Steven's old den and stood back to let him enter. "I don't know how long it's been like this; I never go in there. What were they looking for? Why here?"

"I don't know, Marissa." He didn't touch anything, just walked around making notes on a pad. "Is anything missing?"

"I…I don't know. When I found it like this I panicked and called the police right away." She stepped inside the room and looked closer. She reached down and picked up the end of a power cord. "They took Steven's laptop."

"Was any other room gone through?"

"Not that I noticed. I wasn't paying much attention when I got home."

"You stay here, I'll check it out."

"Marissa!" Lexie bolted down the hall and wrapped her friend in her arms. "Thank God you're okay."

"Lex, I told you not to come," Jordan scolded, a knowing smile on his face. "Yet I was wondering what took you so long."

Lexie hugged Marissa again, before stepping back and smirking at her brother. "You knew you were wasting your breath. I'm not sure why you bothered."

Jordan headed up the stairs to check the rest of the house.

"What happened?" Lexie followed her into the kitchen.

"I don't know exactly," Marissa opened the refrigerator and pulled out a bottle of chardonnay, pouring two glasses before she sat down at the counter. "I went to put the mail in the den and found it completely destroyed."

"Well someone was definitely looking for something." Lexie sipped from her glass. "How scary."

"It doesn't look like anything else has been touched," Jordan said, walking into the kitchen. "But regardless, I want you to come stay with me tonight."

"That's not necessary." Marissa studied him, wondering if he truly wanted her to stay with him or if he was just being polite. "You've been through the house; nobody is lying in wait for me. I'll be fine."

"What's this?" Lexie lifted the envelope from the counter.

"I'm really not sure. I found it in my mailbox today. I don't know who it's from or what it means."

Jordan scowled and examined the envelope, turning it over and back again. "This wasn't mailed, it was hand delivered." He looked sternly at Marissa. "I'm not even going to discuss it with you. Either you pack a bag and come home with me, or I'll find a reason to arrest you, and sleep soundly knowing you're locked away where no one can get to you."

Lexie stood up and patted her brother on the back. "This is why I love you. You're a genius."

Marissa rolled her eyes and sighed. "One night, no more." She left the room to grab a few things and smiled to herself.

Chapter 40

He'd tucked Marissa into his bed and grabbed a pillow and blanket for the couch. He'd noticed the surprise in her eyes, but he wasn't about to be her yo-yo again. He still had some pride left and he planned to hang onto it.

He dialed and waited for Scott to pick up the phone.

"I think I have the evidence you're looking for," he told him, trying to keep his voice down. "But someone else is looking for it, too. They tore through Marissa's house."

"What do you mean you have evidence?" Scott's excitement flowed through the phone.

"Did you hear what I said?" Jordan growled. "They were in her house. What if she would've been home? If anything happens to her…"

"Calm down, nothing is going to happen to her."

"You don't know that. She knows about the juvie record."

"What?" Scott shouted. "How the hell…"

"She received an anonymous note. Hand delivered to her mailbox." Jordan stood and began to pace.

"Tell me about the evidence."

"The anonymous person included photos of Jack with none other than Judge Wallace."

Scott cheered through the phone. "Please tell me you're serious, that you really have these photos."

"I'm serious, I'll drive them down tomorrow." Jordan walked over to the window and looked out at the moon's reflection off the water. "Get that juvie record unsealed. We need to end this. I'm tired of lying and keeping secrets from her. It was bad enough having to keep silent about Steven's other life for close to a damn year because of this case, but now I'm having to lie to her about something almost daily."

Jordan spun around when he heard the front door close. He threw it back open in time to see Marissa step into the elevator. The wind blew from his lungs like he'd been punched. She'd heard him. He had no doubt she'd learned of his deception.

Chapter 41

The fog lingered over the surface of the calm lake as the sun slowly began to rise. The only sounds were the birds chirping, and the occasional plop of a line hitting the water from the small fishing boat. Marissa dangled her feet off the edge of the dock and pulled her sweater tighter.

When she'd left Jordan's last night, she couldn't go home. She didn't want to see him and she didn't think he'd leave her alone.

How could he have done this to her? He'd known about Steven and Jane for a year? Not only had he kept it from her, according to him, he was still lying.

She rubbed her swollen eyes. They burned from the hours she'd spent crying. What if he knew something about Chloe? Something that could bring her daughter home and he hadn't told her? The Jordan she'd thought she knew wouldn't have betrayed her this way.

Her chest felt tight, and she let the tears fall as she realized she'd been made a fool of—again.

* * *

White lines blurred as Jordan weaved in and out of traffic on his way to Los Angeles. Normally, he'd pick his pace, turn up the radio, and enjoy the drive. Today, he needed to get to Scott and close this case. He needed to bring Chloe home to Marissa and beg her to forgive him. He wasn't convinced she ever would, but he'd fight like hell to keep her in his life.

His cell phone rang, interrupting his thoughts. Connecting his Bluetooth he answered his sister's call. "Hey, Lexie, what's up?"

"Is Marissa with you?" she asked.

Lexie was going to strangle him when she found out what he'd done. "No, isn't she home?" Flicking on his blinker, he exited the highway.

"No, she's not, and she's not answering her phone."

He felt a brief moment of panic before reason took over. He was certain she was sitting at the edge of the dock right now with her feet dangling in the water, trying to figure out how he could betray her, too.

"Give her an hour or so and try her back," he instructed. "I bet she went back to the cabin for a while. Maybe you should take Ryan out there. Make a mini vacation out of it, and keep Marissa company." He pulled up at the station. "Let me know when you reach her."

They said their goodbyes and he walked inside to see to Scott. He was surprised to learn he was out of the office for the day. Scott knew he was driving down, so why hadn't he mentioned that important detail?

Jordan slammed his car door in frustration. He didn't want to waste another day in LA. He wanted this wrapped up in a bow and done. He supposed he'd better find a hotel if he was stuck until tomorrow.

Having hit every red light in the thirty or so minutes it'd taken him to get five miles, he was sitting at yet another when he spotted Hamilton walking quickly down the sidewalk.

Crouching lower in his seat to avoid possible detection, Jordan watched him nervously slow down, look behind himself, and quicken his pace again. He slipped into a small convenience store only to leave empty handed a minute or so later. There was no question Hamilton didn't want to be seen, or followed.

The light turned green and Jordan looked for a place to pull in. He had to know where Hamilton was going and what he was up to. As Jordan began to move forward, Hamilton crossed the street with the light, tucking his head down and hunching his shoulders.

The traffic was moving slower than the pedestrians, and Hamilton was halfway down the next block when Jordan got through the intersection.

He pulled into a park and pay lot on the corner of the street. Jordan hopped out of the car as the attendant approached him and shook his head. "We're full, man," the pimple faced youth informed him.

Jordan took a step toward the street and could make out Hamilton crossing to the next block. He was going to lose him. Jordan reached into his wallet and pulled out a fifty dollar bill.

"I need an hour, tops," he said, handing the now salivating attendant the cash. "I'll leave you the keys and when a spot opens, park it for me. Can you do that?"

"Yes, sir." The attendant grinned; never taking his eyes off the money he'd been handed.

Jordan tossed him the keys, pulled a baseball cap from the backseat, pulled it low over his forehead and rushed after his target.

He spotted him two blocks up, still moving at a swift pace but easy to spot as the only person in a jacket with the collar up in the over eighty degree heat. Jordan was able to catch up to him easily, but remained at a distance, stopping occasionally to gaze into a shop window, stoop down to pet a dog on a leash, or slip behind a palm tree.

It didn't matter how many times Hamilton turned to look, Jordan wasn't sure he'd even notice he was being followed. It appeared his nerves might be getting the best of him, and if that were the case, Jordan definitely wanted to know where he was headed.

Hamilton stopped and turned completely around, his head darting from side to side. Jordan sighed with relief when a small table on the sidewalk outside a coffee shop was suddenly vacated and he could smoothly sit. He picked up the empty cup the last customer left and pretended to enjoy the sunshine and a cup of coffee, never taking his eyes off Hamilton.

He tucked his hands in his jacket, lowered his head and slipped around the corner of the building. Jordan rose from his table and again followed Hamilton, who slipped down an alley. With his back pressed up to the building, Jordan slowly peeked around the corner in time to see a door close behind the other cop.

Jordan made sure he was alone and made his way toward the door, opening it just a crack to peer inside. It was obviously the back room to a pawn shop or something similar. He could hear voices and identified Hamilton's easily but couldn't see anyone.

Jordan opened the door a little wider, preparing to step inside when Hamilton came into view of a mirror used to see the lobby from the back room. Closing the door a bit, he made sure he was still able to see the mirror.

Hamilton was handed a bag, but Jordan couldn't see the other man's face. As the men turned to leave, he gasped as Jack Lowell shook Hamilton's hand.

Chapter 42

Marissa sat with Lexie on the porch in the homey wicker chairs outside the cabin while Ryan played catch with his dog, Bell. Marissa watched them, wishing more than ever Chloe was here with her.

She understood why Lexie would drive out to check on her; she was worried and that's what friends did. But she didn't know the latest development and Marissa just wanted to be alone. For the last couple of hours she'd been struggling to find a polite way to ask for her space. The last thing she wanted to be was unappreciative, and everything she came up with sounded rude.

"Jordan's still in LA." Lexie took a sip of her iced tea. "Do you know what he's working on?"

"No idea."

Lexie tilted her head and looked at her suspiciously.

"What? Why are you looking at me like that?"

"What happened?"

"Nothing happened," Marissa insisted.

Lexie turned the chair to face her. "Jordan wouldn't just leave and not contact you at a time like this unless the two of you had a fight."

"We did not have a fight," Marissa raised her voice.

"Well something happened to piss you off."

Marissa wanted to keep insisting nothing had, but Lexie would continue to hound her if she didn't and she hoped once her friend knew about Jordan she'd let her be. She wanted to be alone. She was tired of wearing the fake smile she'd pasted on. "I found out he'd known about Steven for close to a year and never told me."

"What do you mean knew about Steven?" Lexie's face turned red.

"He knew about Steven and Jane, and he kept it from me." She wiped a tear from her cheek.

Lexie pressed her lips together, as if trying to stay silent. "He wouldn't do that," she mumbled.

"I'm serious, Lex." She blew out a frustrated breath. "I heard him on the phone saying he'd known about it for close to a year. He also said he was still lying to me. I didn't stick around to find out what about."

"Mom, Aunt Rissa, look at what Bell can do." Ryan shouted excitedly, throwing the ball so it bounced against the ground and giggling as Bell waited for it to come back down.

Both of them called out their delight in Ryan's newest game before Lexie turned back to her. "He said that?"

Marissa nodded her head. "I don't understand."

Marissa saw the confusion on her friend's face as she seemed to struggle to make sense of it herself. "Why would he do such a thing?"

"I wish I knew."

"He had to have a good reason."

Marissa clenched her teeth and stared at Lexie. "Are you seriously defending him?" she spat.

"No, I'm not defending him, I'm just saying he's not a malicious person, especially when it comes to someone he cares about."

Marissa stood to leave as anger surged through her. She wanted to break something, hit something, anything to release the pressure in her chest. Why did it seem she was constantly trying to convince her friends that there was never a good reason to lie? Lies hurt others, and this time they hurt her. First Steven, now Jordan. The truth was the truth as far as she was concerned. "If that's how he treats someone he cares about, no thank you."

"Marissa, wait." Lexie climbed from the chair. "You have to admit it doesn't add up. Jordan wouldn't keep that to himself unless he thought he had to."

"He thought wrong," she snarled, marching into the cabin and slamming the door.

Chapter 43

"What do you mean his juvenile records are missing?" Jordan shouted.

Scott held up his hands. "Just that, there is nothing in his file. His file is there, but the records aren't."

"So somebody removed them," Jordan said, blowing out a frustrated breath. "Who?"

"It's got to be either Hamilton or Judge Wallace." Scott plopped into the chair behind his desk. "Thanks to you, they're both locked up, so we can get a warrant for their homes, but I doubt we'll find anything."

"Why would Wallace take them?"

"He was the last one to request them before Jack Lowell's trial date. Even though they weren't admitted into evidence, we both know he's read it." Scott slipped off his glasses and rubbed the bridge of his nose. "We don't even know what's in his file, and we don't need it to prosecute him for bribery. So what's the big deal?"

"The big deal is there is more going on here then Lowell bribing a judge to get off on a simple possession charge."

"And paying a cop to make the evidence disappear." Scott nodded. "You're right, but why do you think we'll find the answer in his juvenile file?"

"Two reasons." Jordan held up his fingers. "One, because they're conveniently missing, and two, because someone went to a lot of trouble to make sure Marissa knew about it."

"Either way, they aren't going to simply hand them over."

"The hell they won't!" Jordan gritted his teeth and stormed out of Scott's office.

Thirty minutes later, he jerked his car to a stop outside of the Los Angeles County Jail, and made his way through security.

It took some lying, which he was getting good at, some begging, and a quickly made up excuse, but he was finally granted permission to visit with Judge Wallace.

Jordan paced the small room waiting for the guards to bring him in. When the lock clicked on the other side of the door, he turned to see a distinguished looking gray-haired man in an orange jumpsuit as the guard pushed him into a chair.

"Five minutes," the guard informed him.

Jordan nodded but kept his eyes locked with Wallace's.

"Do I know you?" Wallace asked.

"No, you don't, but I know all about you. I'm Jordan Wayne."

Wallace stared at him for a minute, then asked, "What can I do for you?"

"You can tell me where the juvenile file on Jack Lowell is." Jordan stepped closer, his eyes narrowing as he watched for a reaction.

"I have no idea what you're talking about."

Jordan knew instantly he was lying by the way his eyes broke contact and the movement on his cheeks as he clenched his teeth. "Where are they?"

"If we're done here…" Wallace stood and signaled the guard.

Jordan shook his head, letting the guard know they weren't finished. Rage flowed through his body. He clenched his fists, struggling to gain control of himself. Coming around the table, he pushed the judge back into the chair. "We aren't."

"I don't know what you're talking about," Wallace said again.

"I'm only going to ask you one more time," he spat, each word sounding like its own sentence. "Where is Jack Lowell's juvenile file?"

"I told you, I don't—"

He pictured Chloe, swinging on the play set he'd put up for her, and the look on Marissa's face when she carried her daughter up the stairs to tuck her into bed. He promised her he'd bring

Chloe home, and with all the hurt he'd caused her, this was one promise he had to keep.

Without thought, Jordan reached over the table, grabbed Wallace's hand, and bent his thumb back until it snapped. The judge's eyes grew large and a piercing howl shattered the silence in the room.

"Now, let's try this again…"

Wallace glared up at him. "You can't do this. Do you know who I am?"

A growl escaped his throat as he reached over and took hold of the man's other thumb.

"Okay, okay," Wallace whimpered, flinching. "It's in my wife's office safe."

Jordan stood upright and smiled. "Thank you, you've been very helpful."

Chapter 44

The silence was shattered by a car engine and tires rolling over gravel. Turning around, she felt her heart lurch when she recognized Jordan behind the wheel of the car. She stood and walked toward him.

"Hi," he greeted but avoided eye contact.

"What are you doing here, Jordan?" she asked in a curt tone.

"I need to talk to you," he motioned toward the dock. "Can we?"

She took a deep breath and let it out slowly. She knew he'd reach out to her eventually and try to explain keeping the truth from her, but she wasn't sure she was ready. Her stomach was knotted and tears burned behind her eyes. She refused to let him see her cry over this. Straightening her back defiantly she asked, "Is this about your knowing Steven was having an affair and choosing to keep it from me? I'd rather not discuss that with you right now." She sat at the end of the dock, pulling her legs beneath her.

"It's bigger than that." Looking back across the lake, he ran his hand through his hair.

The silence seemed to stretch for hours as he looked out across the lake. She watched the muscle in his jaw flex and his chest rise and fall with repeated deep breaths.

"I don't need or want your apology, if that's what you've come here to say."

He turned to her, and held her gaze. "I didn't expect you would, but you do need an explanation."

She didn't respond, but sat and waited for him to continue.

"Please try to understand…" he began.

She glared at him, her anger simmering below the surface. "I will never understand. There is no explanation you could give me that would ever make me understand how you, of all people, could do this to me." Tears filled her eyes and she turned away from him.

"Marissa—"

"Jordan, leave me alone. Please," she begged, rising to leave.

He reached out to stop her. "Hear me out. Five minutes and I'll go if that's what you want."

She sat back down, refusing to look at him, she stared across the lake. "Five minutes."

"I found out about Steven and Jane when he got involved in a major case involving his brother."

"Involved how?" She really didn't want to speak to him, but she wanted answers.

"Steven hired an investigator to look into Jack."

"And?" she snapped. "We knew that."

"Let me finish," he said, color seeping into his face.

She turned away again and watched the ripples on the lake.

"Scott Franks, my cop friend in LA, works in internal affairs. When Jack was on trial for possession with intent to sell, something was off. The evidence went missing, the judge wouldn't let any new information be presented, and Hamilton, the cop who made the bust, suddenly wasn't sure he had the right guy."

She listened intently.

"When Jack started blackmailing Steven, he hired an investigator to follow his brother. He couldn't put the pieces together right away but discovered enough that he walked into the department and confronted Hamilton regarding his perjury."

"Where do you come into all of this?" she asked.

"Scott was undercover investigating Hamilton and went to see Steven. After talking to him, he knew exactly who he was and what he was doing, and knowing you and I are friends, he called me to tell me what he could. He wanted me to keep an eye on you. To make sure you were safe."

"So you were spending time with me as a babysitter?"

"You know that's not true."

"I don't know what's true anymore." She shook her head. "You knew all that time Steven was making a fool out of me and you just let it happen."

"I didn't have a choice," he raised his voice. "You know I couldn't tell you."

"No, what I know is you wouldn't. But regardless, why are you telling me all of this now?"

He sighed, almost defeated. "I wanted to tell you personally that Jack Lowell has been arrested, and they've moved the date of your hearing to Monday."

She felt her heartbeat increasing. "So he's in jail? What did he do? Why was he blackmailing Steven, and why would a judge accept a bribe from somebody like Jack? But he can't take Chloe from me, right? Where is she now?"

"She's safe, back with the state until your hearing." He smiled for the first time since he'd arrived. "Do you want to hear this or not?"

"Yes, sorry, continue."

"Jack was a gambler, hence the pictures, but he was in serious debt to some bad people. The judge was the gray-haired man in the photos, and he gambled and was in over his head to the same people."

"Okay, so where does this lead to Jack taking Chloe?"

"Hang on, I'm getting there. The two of them, Jack and Wallace, came up with a scheme to get the money they needed to pay their debts. Wallace told Jack about a large cocaine shipment that was going to be busted, and they figured out how to get their hands on the drugs. Jack then turned around and sold it to his connections. But it went wrong when Hamilton busted Jack and he was arrested."

"So, let me guess, Wallace was the judge on Jack's case?"

"Exactly, and he knew he needed to get Jack off but hadn't planned on the piece of Jack's past that arose when the prosecutor requested his juvenile records unsealed."

"So he did have a juvenile record, like the note said?"

"He did. Remember the picture you found of Steven and Jack as kids and we couldn't figure out who the little girl in the picture was?"

She nodded her head.

"That was Steven's half-sister, Laura. When Jack was a kid, fifteen to be exact, he was a dealer but also a junkie. One night he got high, stole a car with his little sister in tow, and rolled the car, killing her instantly."

She gasped. "Oh no."

"I don't know why Steven never mentioned it, but according to his conversation with Scott, he was filled with hate for his brother, so maybe he just couldn't bring himself to talk about it." He shrugged.

"Maybe…"

"When Jack's juvenile records weren't admitted—which they should've been because they were relevant—and then the drugs he'd been caught with went missing and the arresting officer, Hamilton, changed his story, the prosecutor filed a complaint. That led to an investigation of Judge Wallace. We later found out Hamilton had taken and destroyed the evidence for an easy fifty grand, which I managed to witness the payoff personally."

"And Chloe?"

"When Steven died and Jack learned of the money being left to Chloe, he decided that was his ticket." He shrugged. "Judge Wallace wanted in on this, so they made the juvenile records disappear. So when you went to see Hamilton and mentioned the photos…"

"That's what they were looking for," she said, finally putting it all together. "So what happens to Judge Wallace and Hamilton?"

"Scott arrested Hamilton and turned the evidence over to the FBI, who in turn arrested Wallace." He smiled. "They will both be behind bars for a long time."

"And Jack?"

"The prosecutor has filed a motion to reopen the case due to new evidence, and Jack will also be tried for bribery, paying off a police officer, conspiracy, you name it. He will be behind bars for a long time as well."

"And so Monday?" She rocked back and forth with her knees to her chest, trying to contain her excitement. Not to mention her nervousness.

"Monday, 9 a.m. Your lawyer will meet you there."

He stood to leave and she rose with him. She hugged him and thanked him for informing her of the outcome. She was polite, but knew something had changed between them. The excitement she felt in knowing she had a strong chance of bringing Chloe home was dimmed by the realization that everything she'd feared in loving Jordan had happened. She couldn't trust him. His job as a cop would always have priority, even over her, and for that, she'd resent him. Her heart was broken, and something inside of her had become numb.

She could tell he'd noticed the change as well. His eyes grew dark, his smile faded, and he stepped back. "I should get going," he mumbled. "Good luck on Monday. I hope that everything goes the way it should for both you and Chloe."

"Thank you," she managed as she watched him walk away. *Good bye Jordan,* she thought to herself as she let the tears fall unchecked down her cheeks.

Chapter 45

Marissa flipped through the channels on the television in her hotel room. She needed something to distract her, but this wasn't working. She still had fifteen hours until her hearing and she was unable to sit still. She was sure she'd find a worn path in the carpet by morning.

The knock on the door startled her. She reached to unlock it, and remembered what Jordan had told her. "Who is it?"

"It's Lexie, let me in."

She threw open the door and wrapped her friend in a tight hug. "What are you doing here?"

"I wanted to be here for moral support, and to be with you when you bring Chloe home." She walked into the room and held up a bottle of wine. "Got a corkscrew?"

"You really are a great friend." Marissa smiled in appreciation.

"Because I'm here, or because I brought wine?"

They laughed as Lexie poured Marissa a glass of wine and pulled a bottle of water out for herself.

"I'll be so happy when I can pour two glasses again." She said, and climbed up onto the bed. "I was surprised when Jordan dropped by the house last night." Lexie watched her intently. "I thought he'd be here with you."

She knew her friend was digging for information. "Nope."

"Nope? That's it?" Lexie sputtered.

"He's not here with me, obviously," Marissa watched her friend's expression. She was going to snap, in three, two, one...

"What is going on?" Lexie demanded. "Nobody will tell me anything and it's not right."

Lexie was consistent, that was for sure. "What do you want to know?"

"Are you two riding off into the sunset? Making babies? What?"

Somber, Marissa replied, "No, Lex, we're not."

Lexie actually looked like she might cry. "Why? What happened? I thought you two were doing so good. And please tell me this has nothing to do with his not telling you about Steven."

"Of course it does," Marissa said. Why didn't anyone understand how important honesty was anymore?

"That's ridiculous. You know he was working on a case and couldn't tell you. Don't you think it was eating away at him?"

"Lexie, I don't expect you to understand. I've been lied to, betrayed, and made a fool of too many times. I need to be a priority to him, and I'll always come second to his badge and his code of honor."

"You're a fool."

Marissa felt she'd been slapped.

"Did you know Jordan's been suspended?" Lexie asked smugly.

Her eyes grew large. Suspended?

"For what? That can't be right." Marissa couldn't even fathom Jordan missing a comma on a police report, let alone be suspended.

"He broke an inmate's finger when he wouldn't tell him what he wanted to know." Lexie looked proud.

"What?" Marissa couldn't see it.

"Jordan went to see Judge Wallace to find out where they'd put Jack's juvie record. He wouldn't talk and Jordan made him. Bent his finger back and snapped it."

Marissa shook her head. "No way."

"He did, Marissa, and he did it for you and Chloe. He knew that was the key to put Jack away." She climbed off the bed. "Think about that next time you question his priorities. I'm going to shower."

Marissa couldn't believe it. Jordan had assaulted an inmate to help her? He'd chosen her over the rules, his badge, and his own code of ethics. She'd been wrong all along. She wasn't second place, but she had to learn that not everything could be shared when it came to his job. *I can do that*, she thought, feeling a new surge of hope. Now she had to pray she wasn't too late. It was her turn to apologize and ask for forgiveness for betraying him.

Chapter 46

Marissa paced the hallway outside the courtroom. Lexie and her lawyer, Caroline Dean, seemed as nervous as she was as they waited for the bailiff to let them inside for her custody hearing. She'd called Jordan repeatedly last night, begging him to talk to her, but he hadn't called back. She'd pleaded over his voicemail that she needed him here with her today. Nothing. Every time the elevators opened she held her breath hoping to see him emerge. He still hadn't.

She jerked her head up when the courtroom doors opened and they were ushered inside. Taking her seat beside her attorney, she smiled at the empty table where Jack would've sat.

Jack Lowell's attorney stood and requested a postponement of the trial due to his client's inability to be present. Caroline looked confused but stood to argue the importance of Chloe becoming stabilized.

The judge leaned forward and directed, in a very stern voice, for both attorneys to take their seats.

"There will not be a postponement in this case. Due to the evidence presented to this court, permanent custody of the minor child, Chloe Neil, is granted to Marissa Neil, effective immediately." The judge pounded her gavel.

What just happened? Marissa's head was spinning. She turned to Caroline, who was still staring at the bench with her mouth open.

"Is that it? It's over?" Marissa stuttered. "I can take Chloe home?"

Caroline smiled. "Yes, you can take your daughter home." She turned around, shaking her head as she stuffed papers into her briefcase.

Marissa turned around and beamed at Lexie. "Did you hear that?"

"I did." Lexie stood up and hugged her. "Congratulations, Mama."

Marissa pursed her lips. "Why don't you look surprised? Why are you so calm?"

"I'm not surprised." Lexie shrugged. "Jordan told you he'd bring her home, and he did."

The doors to the courtroom opened and Marissa felt her heart stop as Jordan walked through with Chloe in his arms. A smile lit his face and she wanted to run to them, but she couldn't move. Tears streamed down her cheeks as she watched them coming closer.

Jordan bent down and set Chloe on her feet. Her daughter turned and ran toward her. Marissa scooped her up and pulled her tightly against her.

"Mama," Chloe sang as she wrapped her little arms tightly around her neck.

Marissa had never heard a more beautiful sound. With her baby safely back in her arms, she looked across at Jordan. She had so much she wanted to say to him, but she could only stare, her heart in her eyes.

He walked to her, and she knew by the love in his eyes she hadn't lost him.

"I'm so sorry," she whispered. "I was such a fool. I do trust you, with all that I am, I trust you."

"Dada." Chloe reached out her arms to him.

Jordan reached for her and held her against him with tears rolling down his cheeks.

"I love you, Marissa," Jordan said tenderly. "Since the moment I laid eyes on you, I've loved you."

"I love you, Jordan."

Chloe shifted in his arms, as if she were making room for Marissa. He wrapped his free arm around her shoulder and drew her in for a kiss.

Pulling away breathless, Marissa beamed, unable to contain the overwhelming happiness she felt. "Are you ready to be a dad?"

"I already feel like her dad." Jordan kissed Chloe's cheek.

Jordan wrapped his arm around her. "Let's go home."

As they turned to leave, Lexie gasped. Her eyes grew wide as she stared at the puddle of water beneath her feet.

Marissa looked at her friend and smiled. "Jordan, we're going to have to make a stop on the way home."

Racing into action, Jordan handed Chloe to Marissa and wrapped his arm around his sister leading her from the courtroom. He smiled, and turned back to Marissa, "Pay attention because if I have my way, this will be you in say, nine months."

Marissa kissed his lips softly and beamed at him as they walked side by side into their future.

About the Author

Erin McCauley resides in the Pacific Northwest with her three children, writing deeply moving love stories that will have you believing in happily ever after. You can visit her website at *www. erinmccauley.com*.

More from This Author
(from *The Truth* by Erin McCauley)

Lexie Wayne looked down at the tombstone and fought back the tears as Ryan bent down to place the bouquet of daisies on his mother's grave. The rain fell as if the sky wept for them. She adjusted the umbrella to shield them from the pelting drops.

"Do you think she sees us?" Ryan looked into her eyes as only an inquisitive four-year-old can.

"I think so, yes." She laid her arm across his shoulders in comfort.

"How come she left?" he asked, not for the first time.

"It wasn't her choice, Ryan. If she could have stayed with you forever, she would have." Looking into his innocent face, her eyes pooled with tears.

"But why?"

"God needed her with him, and He knew you and I would be okay, just the two of us," she answered, unable to contain the tears now rolling down her cheeks.

"How come he needed her?"

She searched for the words to explain the unexplainable. "Your mother was so special that God needed her to be a big angel and watch over a lot of people, instead of a mommy to look over only a few."

"So why are you only a mommy and not an angel? You're special, right?"

She ruffled his dark curls. "I'm not quite ready for that big of a responsibility. Besides, I believe you and I were meant to be together. Everything happens for a reason, even if we don't understand why."

"What's res- respons-?"

Lexie smiled, crouched down, and pulled him onto her lap. "Responsibility? Well, it means taking care of something big, something important."

Ryan narrowed his eyes, his lips pursed in thought. "So, God didn't need you to be an angel, but he needed you to be my mommy?"

"Exactly." Her heart swelled and she pulled him closer to her.

"I'm glad." He snuggled into her. "I'm glad you're my mommy."

She held onto him for a minute, closed her eyes, and basked in the feeling of his warm breath against her chest, and the comfort of his small arms wrapped around her. Placing a kiss on his temple, she stared at the tombstone of her friend. "Me, too, baby. Me, too."

Lexie had met his mother, Maggie, when she'd come to work for her at the coffee shop. They became fast friends and Lexie was the one to check her into Nathan's Hope Hospice House when her cancer had become untreatable. She had succumbed to the disease three years ago. Maggie would have been twenty-eight years old today, the same age Lexie turned just last month. She felt a tear slide down her cheek at the unfairness of it all. Lexie still missed her, but the life she'd discovered since moving Ryan into her home had become all-encompassing.

They stood in silence for a moment as the rain continued to fall, then Lexie took Ryan's hand and they began to walk across the grass. Lured by another gravesite beneath a large palm tree, she felt compelled to stop. Pulled forward by a force she hadn't felt in years, she knelt and gently ran her hand over the top of the smooth granite, now glistening with water.

"Your favorite kind of day," she smiled wistfully as she spoke to the stone. "Wet, but warm, with a strong chance of a rainbow."

"Who are you talking to?" Ryan knelt alongside her.

She straightened and pulled him to his feet. "An old friend," she managed to say, forcing the words through her constricted throat.

"Is your friend an angel like my mommy?"

Squeezing his hand, Lexie nodded her head as the tears ran down her cheeks. "One of the most important angels of all. He always was." She took a deep breath and blew it out slowly through pursed lips, and wiped the tears from her cheeks.

Turning to her son, she felt her love for him surge through her. "You want to go to work with me today?"

He grinned and nodded his head so fast it caused him to lose his balance. "Can I wear an apron, too?"

"Absolutely," she said. Locking away her sorrow, she forced a smile to her lips. "You must be in uniform if you're going to be serving the customers."

Tugging her hand, he dragged her across the grass toward the car.

Ryan bounced in his seat, unable to contain his excitement as they pulled into the parking lot outside of Lexie's coffee shop, Ocean Breeze Java. The car was barely in park when Ryan spotted his uncle through the window and tugged off his seatbelt before wrestling with the door handle. Ryan landed with a splash in a large puddle in his haste to get out of the car, chanting "Uncle Jordan, Uncle Jordan!" as he ran toward the shop.

Lexie rushed around the car and caught Ryan's hand, pulling him onto the sidewalk before another car whipped into the open parking spot beside them. Escaping her grasp, he scampered ahead of her.

"Ryan, slow down, wait for me!" She fumbled with the key, struggling to lock the car before she rushed after him. "Ryan, come here."

Ignoring her call, Ryan raced around the man who held open the coffee shop's glass door. Thrown off balance by the boy zipping past him, the man twisted, struggling to maintain his footing.

Foreseeing the disaster about to happen, Lexie grabbed for the door in an attempt to stop it from slamming into the man. The strap of her purse slipped from her shoulder and spilled its contents on the cement.

Like a slow-motion scene in a bad comedy, Lexie's left foot came down hard on a tube of lip gloss and shot out from under her. She pin-wheeled her arms and struggled to regain her footing, resembling an amateur log roller. Unable to catch her balance, she latched onto the only thing close enough to grab — the already off-balance man in the doorway.

Pulling him down with her, the weight of his body slammed her to the sidewalk causing cartoon stars to whirl about her head and all the air to explode from her lungs in a large whoosh. She blinked her eyes and tried to get them to focus. She was currently seeing three and four identical things, all in different distortions.

She regained focus and looked up into intense green eyes, with the longest black eyelashes she'd ever seen. Skimming down, her eyes followed the path of a small bump on an otherwise straight nose splattered with a light trace of freckles. Strong cheekbones supported a shadow of dark whiskers. She felt the heat rise on her cheeks as her eyes fixated on his mouth and the smirk on his perfectly sculpted face.

Attempting to rise on her elbows, she realized he was lying across the entire length of her body, supporting his weight on one elbow like a lover basking in the afterglow.

Humiliated, she frowned and cocked her head. "Do you mind?"

"Not at all," he said, as the dimples in his cheeks deepened.

He placed his hands on the ground on either side of her head and lowered his face directly above hers. Her heart pounded in anticipation, her mind lost all thought, and she ran her tongue across her lips. But in one quick motion, he pushed off his arms and landed on his feet. With a mischievous grin, he held his hand out to her. "Here, let me help you."

Lexie felt her cheeks flush in embarrassment as she pictured how foolish she must look. She glared up at him and, ignoring his outstretched hand, sat up and picked up the contents of her purse. Determined to save what was left of her dignity, she stood, straightened her shirt, brushed off her knees like she was wearing Gucci instead of old jeans, and ran her hand through her hair. She pulled her shoulders back and stuck her chin out in defiance.

Stepping around the insolent man, Lexie came face to face with her brother, Jordan, who stood watching the scene with uncontained amusement. Beside him, Ryan stood in silence with his head hung low, gripping his uncle's hand.

"Sorry, Mommy," he whispered to the floor.

"This wasn't exactly the introduction I had in mind when I brought him over here," Jordan said, biting back a laugh, "but Lexie, I'd like you to meet my new partner, Deputy Grayson Hunter."

Lexie turned around and locked eyes with the man, who was still wearing a self-satisfied grin, and groaned. "Perfect," she mumbled, "just perfect."

"Grayson, I see you've met my sister, Lexie. And this little speed demon is my nephew, Ryan."

Lexie clenched her teeth together. She wanted nothing more than to wipe the smirk from Grayson Hunter's handsome, chiseled face. Her body still hummed from the anticipation of his almost-kiss. Her hands itched to trace the lines of his face, to bury them in his thick black hair. She didn't like it. What she liked less was that her response had been noticed. Grayson's eyes shone with the spark of challenge.

She clasped her hands together, smiled sweetly, and batted her eyes mockingly. "New partner? Oh, that's such good news. The only thing missing from this town is a cop who's light on his feet and as graceful as a one-legged tap dancer."

Jordan groaned.

Grayson's eyes flashed with mischief. "You can't blame a man for being swept off his feet by a beautiful woman."

"Should we worry when he's swept off his feet by a four-year-old boy?" Lexie challenged.

Grayson ignored her retort, and held out his hand to Ryan. "It's nice to meet you."

Ryan giggled and reached out to shake the outstretched hand.

He stepped through the door behind a laughing Jordan and turned around, his eyes filled with amusement. "And Lexie, it was very nice bumping into you."

In the mood for more Crimson Romance?
Check out *Slow Ride* by Kat Morrisey at *CrimsonRomance.com*.